There, On Th Was His Name, Brey Angell.

He stared at it, hardly breathing.

He could erase it with the stroke of a key. No one was looking. It would take only seconds and he could wipe out the record, make sure no one ever knew. He glanced back into the nursery, craned his head to see baby Calli's bed. The only things visible from this angle were her little fists waving in the air. His heart lurched and he shook his head, looking back at the screen.

No. He wouldn't erase his name. He was Calli's father, and no one would ever be able to take that away from him.

Dear Reader,

Happy holidays from the staff at Silhouette Desire! As you can see by the special cover treatment this month, these books are our holiday gifts to you. And each and every story is so wonderful that I know you'll want to buy extras to give to your friends!

We begin with Jackie Merritt's MAN OF THE MONTH, *Montana Christmas*, which is the conclusion of her spectacular MADE IN MONTANA series. The fun continues with *Instant Dad*, the final installment in Raye Morgan's popular series THE BABY SHOWER.

Suzannah Davis's *Gabriel's Bride* is a classic— and sensuous—love story you're sure to love. And Anne Eames's delightful writing style is highlighted to perfection in *Christmas Elopement*. For a story that will make you feel all the warmth and goodwill of the holiday season, don't miss Kate Little's *Jingle Bell Baby*.

And Susan Connell begins a new miniseries— THE GIRLS MOST LIKELY TO... —about three former high school friends who are now all grown up in *Rebel's Spirit*. Look for upcoming books in the series in 1997.

Happy holidays and happy reading from

Lucia Macro

AND THE STAFF OF SILHOUETTE DESIRE

Please address questions and book requests to:
Silhouette Reader Service
U.S.: 3010 Walden Ave., P.O. Box 1325, Buffalo, NY 14269
Canadian: P.O. Box 609, Fort Erie, Ont. L2A 5X3

RAYE MORGAN
INSTANT DAD

SILHOUETTE *Desire*®
Published by Silhouette Books
America's Publisher of Contemporary Romance

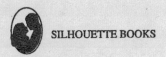 SILHOUETTE BOOKS

ISBN 0-373-76040-X

INSTANT DAD

RAYE MORGAN

favors settings in the West, which is where she has spent most of her life. She admits to a penchant for Western heroes, believing that whether he's a rugged outdoorsman or a smooth city sophisticate, he tends to have a streak of wildness that the romantic heroine can't resist taming. She's been married to one of those Western men for twenty years and is busy raising four more in her Southern California home.

Prologue

THE INVITATIONS ARE OUT

"**W**hy do they call them baby showers, anyway?"

Sara Parker looked up from the last of the invitations she was addressing. "I don't know. Maybe because they are a celebration where you shower the baby with gifts."

"Hmm." Jenny Kirkland sounded skeptical. Leaning back in her chair, she patted her rounded belly. "I just hope this little one arrives in time for the shower you're having. It'll be fun for you to show all your friends your new baby."

Sara glanced at where her sister's hand was placed, an uneasy mixture of love and envy filling her eyes. If only she were the one who was pregnant instead of Jenny, this would all seem more natural. But no matter—the baby Jenny was carrying would soon be hers. It was the waiting that was so hard.

"You're invited too, you know," she said with a quick smile.

Jenny laughed. "I don't think so. Baby showers and a bunch of women getting together to play games and drink green punch are not exactly my sort of scene."

Sara knew she was only being honest. Jenny could usually be found wherever the music was the loudest and the men the handsomest. It was amazing that Sara had been able to convince her to spend all these months gestating a baby and she knew Jenny was champing at the bit to get back into the action on the singles scene.

"Only a couple more weeks," she told her softly as she put the stamp on the last envelope. "Not long at all."

Jenny stared at her for a moment, her green eyes rebellious. But she didn't express what she was thinking. Instead, she sighed and said, "Let's go over it again. If it's a girl, I'll name her Calli. If it's a boy, I'll name him Christopher. Is that it?"

Sara nodded. Those were the names they had decided upon between them. Jenny had been particularly keen on the boy's name and that made Sara wonder.

"Was his name Christopher?" she asked casually, still sealing envelopes.

Jenny looked up, startled. "Whose name?"

"You know who I mean. The baby's father."

Jenny rolled her eyes. "Oh, please. Let's not get sentimental about this." She tossed her red hair back over her shoulder, then glanced at her sister's face and softened when she saw the look in her eyes. "Oh, forget about it, Sara. You don't want to know who the father was. It's better left alone."

But Sara did want to know. She hated leaving strings, leaving things undone, unfinished. "But if he shows up all of a sudden and wants his child."

"He won't. He doesn't even know I'm pregnant. He'll never know."

Sara wanted to say more, but she held her tongue. She and Jenny might be sisters, but they were very different and didn't often see eye to eye on anything. Where Sara wanted the *i*s dotted and the *t*s crossed, Jenny wouldn't even bother to write out full words. Abbreviations would do for her.

"You're not having second thoughts, are you?" Jenny asked suddenly.

"Me?" Sara stared at her. "That'll be the day. I can hardly wait to…" Her eyes filled with dreams and her voice lowered. "To hold the little bundle in my arms and kiss that downy head and—"

"Okay, okay," Jenny said quickly. "I get the picture." She pushed herself awkwardly out of the chair and rose, turning in the direction of the kitchen. "I can hardly wait, either. Only with me, it's like waiting to get out of prison. Once I deliver this child, I'll be free, and you can bet I'll never get myself in this condition again."

Sara sighed as her sister disappeared down the hallway. She'd done all she could for the past few months, trying to keep Jenny's spirits up, trying to get her to rest and eat well. For a while, she'd even had her living here in her house so that she could keep an eye on her. But they'd clashed a few too many times and Jenny had gone back to her apartment. Now she came by to visit every few days, but that was it. And Sara was feeling very much alone in her adventure.

That was why she wanted her friends around her so badly. She spread out the invitations on the desk, looking for the most important ones. She'd invited people from all over, but there were only three she really cared about—her three roommates from college. She hadn't seen any of them for almost ten years and she felt that lack like an ache in her heart.

There was warm, lovable Cami Bishop, now publishing a fern journal in California. Hailey Kingston, beautiful as any model, had come back from art school in Paris to begin a career as a buyer for a San Francisco department store. And J. J. Jensen was in Utah, from what she'd heard, still pursuing her dream of landing the anchor position on some big network television news show. The four of them had been inseparable all through college, there for secrets and for comfort, helping each other pass exams and heal broken hearts. They had all been so full of dreams when they'd started out. Funny how none of the goals had quite panned out. Still, those three young women had been responsible for pulling her away from the defensive, introspective world she'd built around her like a cocoon since childhood, pulling her away from that out into the sunshine. She would always love them for it. Now she felt herself losing confidence again and she needed her old roommates' help to get through this.

"Please come," she whispered as she tied the envelopes together and prepared for a trip to the post office. "The way things are going, I have a feeling I'm really going to need a friend."

One

Drey Angeli walked into the colorful Denver steak house like a man who knew what he wanted. The place had elk hides on the wall and long horns mounted over the bar. With his shoulder-length golden hair and buckskin jacket worn to the color of sandstone in the sun, Drey looked as if he belonged there.

Stopping for a moment to let his eyes adjust to the dim light, he shook his head at the scantily clad hostess hurrying toward him and surveyed the clientele on his own. He spotted the man he was looking for and started toward him. At six foot four with shoulders as wide as an acre of land, he made an imposing figure and people tended to make way when they saw him coming.

"Hello, Carter," he said, stopping at a table where a tall, thin man sat devouring a thick porterhouse. "I've been looking for you."

The older man looked up, did a double take and grinned. "Sit down, Drey," he said, waving an invitation to the opposite chair. "I haven't seen you since you ran off with my wife. Sit down and fill me in on what's been happening."

Drey slid into the seat in one fluid motion and reached for Carter's drink, taking a sip and making a face.

"Still drinking rotgut, I see."

Signaling the waitress, he put in an order for bourbon and water, then turned and gazed at his companion with his head back and his eyes half-closed. "I didn't, you know," he said quietly.

Carter stared at him for a long moment before saying, "Run off with Nancy?" He shrugged and began cutting off another huge bite of meat. "Let's just say she went running after you."

Drey waited a moment, thinking while Carter chewed. Finally he responded. "Your wife," he said, choosing his words deliberately, "was hardly in a rational frame of mind when she left you. She just needed some time."

"Hey, Drey, it's okay." Carter laughed softly, reaching for his napkin and wiping his mouth before he took another sip of his drink. "She's back home where she belongs. She told me how you talked her into coming back to me. Everything's cool. I was ribbing you."

Relief filled Drey's dark eyes for a moment and he took a deep breath. "I'm glad, Carter. For your sake and for mine." He hesitated, then went on. "I've got a favor to ask you."

The waitress brought his drink and he knocked back a portion of it, then sat for a moment, letting it warm him inside. "Here's the deal. I hear you have a woman named Sara Parker asking you to find her a carpenter to put in some shelves and do some cabinetry work."

Carter nodded slowly, waiting.

Drey met his gaze and held it. "Send me," he said simply.

Carter's eyebrows rose. "You? You haven't worked for me since you graduated college. What was that? Five years ago?"

Drey nodded. "Let me take it, Carter. I don't care about the money. You can have it all. I just want to go out there and do the job."

Carter's eyes narrowed as he speculated. "What's going on, Drey? What's your relationship with the lady? You got the hots for her or something?"

Drey shook his head. "I've never met her. But I want to do the job. I've got my own reasons."

Carter hesitated, puzzled. "I don't know," he said slowly. "How long's it been since you've done any work with wood?"

Drey let out a hiss of exasperation. "Give me a break. You don't think I'd do a good job?"

Carter laughed softly. "Nah, I always did say you were the best carpenter I ever hired."

Drey nodded, as though that settled it, and took a long sip of his bourbon. "Tell me something," he said, leaning a little closer. "You've worked for this woman before, haven't you? Where's Mr. Parker?"

Carter shrugged, still watching Drey as though he were trying to figure him out. "I haven't ever seen him. He's always away on business trips. He's some sort of high-class executive or something."

Drey contemplated that for a moment, frowning. "You've done a lot of work out at her place?"

Carter grimaced. "Not a lot. I got a pool house built for her last summer and fixed a couple of doors that were sticking. Oh, and we made her an enclosure for her microwave. That's about it."

Drey nodded slowly.

Carter leaned forward, curiosity burning in his eyes. "Come on, Drey. Give. What's going on?"

Drey's smile was faint but evident. "It's personal."

Carter frowned, staring at him. "It may be personal to you, but it's business to me. I've got to be sure you're on the up-and-up here, Drey. Mrs. Parker is a good client of mine."

Drey's mouth twisted as he thought over his options. "Okay," he said at last. "I'll tell you this much. I used to date her sister, Jenny Kirkland."

Carter stared at him. "What is this, Drey? Did she dump you?"

Drey allowed himself a fleeting smile. "No, she didn't dump me."

"Did you dump her?"

Drey's mouth gave a quirk of annoyance. "That doesn't matter. Do I get the job or not?"

Carter shook his head, his eyes troubled. "I don't know. Something doesn't smell right here."

Drey shrugged, gazing at him coolly. "You've known me for a long time. Do you trust me or don't you?"

Carter shook his head and, finally, he grinned reluctantly. "Hell, I trusted you with my wife, didn't I? I guess I can trust you with Sara Parker."

"Good," Drey said, nodding slowly, his gaze already on a distant scene. "Good."

Drey vaulted out of his four-wheel drive, all-terrain vehicle and reached for his tool belt, then gazed at

Sara Parker's gabled and turreted house with a healthy
dose of skepticism. What kind of woman would live
in a place like this? She either had to be an impris-
oned princess or the wicked witch of the north. There
weren't many other options.

Making his way up the walk, he glanced up and
down the street. The area houses were large and dis-
tinctive, the yards professionally trimmed and
sculpted. The neighborhood reeked of money.

It was late afternoon and the breeze had turned
frosty. He knew he wouldn't get much work done today, but he could take measurements and scope the
situation out. He figured on being here for the rest of
the week if things worked out the way he'd planned.

A bouquet of spring flowers sat in a cheap glass vase
on the doorstep. He glanced down at it, then rang the
bell. There was no answer, and he reached down to
pick up the flowers and look at the card.

"Sara, darling, so sorry, but I'm not going to be
able to make it to your baby shower. Hope these
flowers will make it up to you. Kiss kiss, love Sylvia."

"Baby shower," he repeated softly out loud. That
would seem to confirm what he'd heard. Sara Parker
was adopting Jenny Kirkland's baby.

The sound of tires on the driveway brought his head
around and he watched as the expensive silver sedan
pulled to a stop and a tall, blond woman swung her
long legs out, then rose to look at him.

He stood where he was, not moving, and she pushed
the car door shut, then came walking toward him. She
was dressed in a powder pink cashmere suit and soft
leather shoes with trendy heels. Her blond hair was
pulled back in an elegant twist at the nape of her neck.
Gold bracelets flashed at her wrists, gold and dia-

monds sparkled on her fingers, and her nails were painted a perfect match to the suit.

In fact, everything about her seemed just about perfect. The only thing missing, he thought as she came close enough to see into her crystal blue eyes, was passion. There was no passion, no anger, no joy, no fear visible in her face. She might have been cut from ice. She was an ice lady, very cool, very calm, and very much in control.

And very confident. Some women might have hesitated upon seeing a man who looked like him standing on their front step. He knew his long hair and jeans and buckskin jacket looked out of place here in this part of town. A lot of people gave him a second look because of it, but he didn't care. He considered his look consistent with the history of Denver. Jenny used to tell him he looked like a nineteenth-century miner, only cleaner and healthier.

"Wild and woolly," she would say, laughing at him.

But his wild look didn't seem to bother Ms. Parker. She came up to him like the home owner she was, sure of herself and of whose property they were standing on.

"I'll take those," she said calmly, reaching out her hand for the flowers. "If you'll wait just a moment, I'll give you something."

So that was it. She thought he was there to bring her flowers.

"I'm not a delivery boy," he told her, handing the arrangement over as though the posies had suddenly developed thorns. "They were on your doorstep when I got here."

"Oh." She glanced at him, wondering why he hadn't left them there, and he saw the question in her eyes, but he ignored it.

"I'm from Carter Construction," he said quickly. "I'm here to do some carpentry work you needed."

"Oh." She actually smiled and it lit her face. "Thank goodness. We've got a lot of work to get done in a short time. Please come in."

Their eyes met for just an instant and they both pulled back, as though a spark of static electricity had sprung between them. He almost thought that must have been it. The air was dry and it was cold. Perfect weather for static electricity.

He followed her into the house, his boots marking time on the marble entryway, then waited while she put her things away in the kitchen. From where he stood, he could see into the living room with its glass-and-wood furniture, its overstuffed couch and granite fireplace, into the den where glass-faced bookcases filled with volumes lined the walls, and into the kitchen where the lady was putting her purse under the counter and checking her answering machine.

He frowned. The place was all angles and hard surfaces. If she thought she was going to adopt a baby, she was going to have to do something about that. This was not a baby-proof environment. He was going to have to find an opportunity to point that out to her.

"I didn't get your name," she noted as she returned to him.

"Drey Angeli," he said, glancing down at the small, slim hand she held out before taking it in his own. Her grip was firm but her hand felt as soft and elegant as it looked.

"I guess you know I'm Sara Parker," she said. "I'm so glad you've come so promptly."

He raised one eyebrow, wondering why she was treating him like his sixth-grade schoolteacher, the one who always corrected his grammar and held him after school for being a smart aleck. Instinctively he knew she did it on purpose. But what that purpose was, he couldn't imagine.

"Follow me," she said crisply, turning to lead him through the foyer. "I'll show you where I'm going to need the work done."

He followed her, noting the way her every movement seemed to be according to some careful plan. Her step was quick and light and very determined, and when she started up the stairs in front of him, he couldn't keep from watching the nice way her bottom swayed in the pink cashmere skirt, and something about that experience made him study her face when she reached the top and turned to wait for him.

His first impression had been of her coldness, but now that he gave her a second look, he realized she was quite pretty. Her features were small and fine as porcelain, her skin smooth, her eyes a brilliant, starburst blue set off by thick black lashes. He had the sudden picture of a ballerina in his mind, an old-fashioned dancer mincing in toe shoes with her arms raised in position.

"This way," she told him, turning and leading him into a room off the hallway.

He followed her, only half listening while she detailed the new closet space she wanted in the guest bedroom. He was studying the room for evidence. Just what sort of woman was Sara Parker?

She was certainly a contrast to her sister, but then, he'd already known that, hadn't he? Jenny had told him so.

"She's not like the rest of our family," Jenny had told him one night over drinks at a lodge at the lake. "When we were kids, we called her Stuck-up Sara. Do you know she actually packaged her dolls in plastic wrap and buried them in the backyard so the rest of us wouldn't play with them?"

Drey remembered gazing at Jenny that evening, bemused, wondering why her voice was trembling with annoyance so many years later.

"And when we were teenagers, forget it. She kept her side of the room roped off so I wouldn't touch her things, and she taped hairs to her dresser drawers so she could tell when I went through them." Jenny's pretty heart-shaped face flushed. "We didn't get along."

No, he could see that Jenny would have a hard time getting along with this exquisite creature. Jenny was casual about clothes, plans, men. She was open and generous and free spirited—but she was also careless and petulant at times. Sara Parker didn't seem to be any of the above.

Everything about her was careful; everything matched, from her fingernail polish to her creamy lipstick to the pink cloisonné comb that held her silver blond hair in place.

She cares too much, he thought to himself. Wasn't that a sign of some sort of neurosis?

"Now down here," she said, leading him to another room down the hall. "Here is the nursery. I'm going to need new shelves and a set of waist-high cabinets. I'd like to install a changing table here, as well."

He nodded. "Do you have any children?" he asked, wondering if Jenny's baby was going to be an only child.

"Not yet." She actually smiled. "But I'm about to have a baby."

"Really?" He knew she was expecting him to glance at her flat stomach in surprise, so he did. "Not anytime soon."

"Yes. Very soon. Sometime in the next two weeks, in fact." She laughed softly and her starry eyes seemed to melt into pools of silver. "I'm adopting."

He waited a moment but she didn't say it. He knew she was adopting her sister's baby. Why not mention that? Why not talk about the fact that this was Jenny's baby? Or was that some sort of secret she was keeping?

But she didn't mention it. Instead, she gave him a smile that startled him. "You don't know how much I appreciate you showing up," she said. "You're the only one. I've called an electrician, a landscaper and a pool maintenance man and you're the only one who came when you said you would."

He frowned, a defense against the smile. He didn't want to like her.

"You've filled your pool already?" he noted, looking out the window at the forest behind the house. "Isn't it a bit early?"

"Oh, I don't think so." She turned slowly, looking the room over as if to make sure she wasn't forgetting to tell him anything about the job. "The weather has been so warm. And I need it filled. It looks so much better that way and I'm having a party next week. A baby shower. I need everything to look perfect."

Perfect. Yeah, that was what she wanted. It showed.

"I'll bet you ten to one we get another snowstorm before the season's over," he said, trying to burst her bubble.

But she was having none of it. Shaking her head, she smiled at him again. "No, absolutely not. No snowstorm. Spring is here."

She walked over to her window and gestured out into her backyard where birds were chirping in the trees. "Look at all those birds. Would they be here if snow was coming?"

He followed her, then stood by her side, looking down. There were birds all right. Flocks of them. "You think birds have an inside track on the weather?" he grumbled.

"No, not really." She frowned, considering, and he noticed her delicate eyebrows. She didn't pluck them. She didn't have to. They were perfect.

"But are you trying to tell me there's no order in the universe?" she asked him, sighing softly. "That it's *all* anarchy?" Her eyes clouded.

He felt a twinge of remorse. It was pretty obvious she needed order to feel secure. There was no reason to be so churlish, he supposed. She hadn't done anything to him. Not yet, anyway.

"I wouldn't go that far," he admitted gruffly. "But I don't think birds know all that much more than we do about it."

She was still staring at him as though she were hoping to find some kind of answer in his eyes, and he moved uncomfortably, trying to avoid her gaze but unable to look away himself.

"They have instincts," she said as though she'd just thought of it.

He shrugged. Why did this seem to be so important to her? "So do we," he muttered, tearing his gaze away and scowling out the window.

She laughed softly, turning away, as well. "You're right. I'm sorry. I get carried away with these things sometimes."

Afraid that she'd embarrassed him by getting a little too familiar, she glanced back. He was still frowning. His face, the set of his shoulders, everything said *don't tread on me,* and she suppressed a smile. He was a good-looking man in his way, though she hadn't noticed at first. Probably because of the long hair. But he was certainly a strong-looking man, his hands square and chiseled, his shoulders wide and western. He could have been a cowboy riding into Denver a hundred years ago, or a miner coming in off the high country with a sack of gold in his belt.

A throwback, she thought to herself. In this high-tech age you didn't see many like him any longer.

"Never mind," she said quickly, hoping to put him at ease. "I'll get going."

She headed for the door, her handmade leather shoes sinking into the plush carpeting. "I'll leave you to your measuring and your plans. Please let me see what you've worked out when you're finished. I'll be downstairs."

"Sure will," he said, watching her go, but she didn't turn or smile or anything. She just kept going, and then she was gone.

He swore softly to himself. He hadn't figured her out yet and he'd thought it was going to be easy. From what Jenny had told him, he'd expected to find a cold fish with rigid views, a sort of wicked witch of the Rockies. He'd been prepared to despise her. Obviously the judgment wasn't that simple. Still, there was time. There was plenty of time. From what he'd been able to find out, Jenny's baby wasn't due for another week or so. He would have to make a decision by then.

Meanwhile, he had some woodworking to do.

and the weather was fine . . . .

time. Going up inside of a . . .
up to the old brick . . .
watched for . . .
footstep . . .

Two

—

Sara glanced upstairs. She could hear the carpenter
moving something in the baby's room and she hesitated, tempted to run up and see what was going on.
But she thought better of it. Let him finish his work.
She had things of her own to accomplish.

The baby shower was only a little over a week away
and the planning was as meticulous as though she were
leading an army into battle. She'd made lists and set
timers and ordered things, but the work was never
ending. At the moment, she'd changed into slacks and
a sweater and she was checking items off the latest list.

"Windows. The window washer came this morning. That's done. The chimney sweep came last Saturday. The gardener still needs to put in the pansies
and petunias. The painter says he's coming tomorrow
to touch up the trim on the house."

There were still so many things to fix or clean or renovate before next week. One thing was that darn pool. She'd had the gardener take the cover off for her, and the pool man had said he would be here by noon. That was five hours ago. He obviously wasn't coming.

Glancing out at it, she frowned. The gardener had gone home and there was the pool, starting to collect leaves on its surface. She couldn't just leave the cover there. It looked so ugly. Besides, there was a breeze and she was afraid things would blow into the pool during the night. Better to get it covered again.

She looked toward the stairs, knowing she could get the carpenter to come help her with the cover. But he was busy, and the cover was a simple affair. She should be able to do it herself.

Armed with all her self-confidence, she marched out through her sliding glass doors and onto the pool deck. The air was brisk on her skin and she rubbed her arms, wishing she'd put on a jacket. But this should be quick. The cover was made of plastic bubble sheeting and it was actually quite light. Grasping one edge, she began to pull it over the pool water.

It went easily at first, sliding along so well she looked back, pleased. But just as she did, the cover caught on the stair railing and gave a sudden snap of resistance, throwing her off balance. With a cry, she took a bad step and the next thing she knew, she was falling into the water.

The water was cold, so cold it might have been just one level below ice. It seemed to crash around her like a wave in the ocean, hard and awful, stunning her, knocking her breath away. She tried to cry out again, but her mouth was full of water, and her eyes were full

of water, and the cover seemed to be looming up above
her, over the water, and she seemed to be closing her
eyes.

But only for a second or two. Suddenly, strong
hands were gripping her arms and she was shooting
back up through the icy water, up into what was left
of the sunshine.

She gasped for air, her system in cold shock, hardly
realizing that Drey had pulled her up into his arms and
was striding quickly into the house, with water spill-
ing off her in every direction.

"Oh," she gasped. "Oh, that was so cold!"

"Hang on," he said as he carried her up the stairs.
"We'll get you warm again."

The next thing she knew, she was in her spacious
bathroom and he was turning on the water for the
shower in the bathtub. She wanted to ask what he was
doing, but her teeth were chattering so hard she
couldn't get the words out. Her clothes hung on her
like sodden armor, heavy and cold. Drey turned from
the bathtub and began to remove them.

"No!" she cried, or tried to, but he didn't listen.

"Don't be stupid," he said bluntly, taking a grip on
her sweater and beginning to tug it up over her head
the way he might have done with a child. "You've got
to get warm and you've got to do it now."

She knew he was right, and in the state she was in at
the moment, she wasn't sure she was capable of taking care of this on her own. So she bit back her pro-
tests and closed her eyes.

He stripped her quickly, dropping the wet clothes to
the floor, and turned to test the water coming out of
the shower nozzle, then led her into the enclosure,
helping her over the side of the tub.

"Stand under the water until you get enough in the tub to sit in," he ordered her. "Then sit. You've got to soak warmth back into your body."

The warm water stung at first. She gasped again, turning under it, hardly feeling modest about the fact that she was standing there naked in front of this stranger. The cold was more important than her dignity right now. Besides, there was nothing in his eyes that even hinted at a sensual response of any kind. He was as grim faced as a medical worker at the scene of the accident, no emotion in sight. As that realization hit her, she wasn't sure if she was grateful or insulted. As he turned to leave the room, she looked after him.

"Where are you going?" she asked, almost anxious. After all, he'd saved her, hadn't he?

"Who's your doctor?" he asked, turning at the doorway. "I'll call him."

"No," she said quickly. "No, don't call a doctor. I'm fine. Really."

And she was beginning to feel like herself again, enough so that she pulled the glass door of the shower almost closed as a shield to hide behind. For the first time, she looked at him and really saw him.

"You're soaking wet," she cried, looking at his dripping clothes. "Did you actually jump in after me?"

He shook his head and gave her a faint lopsided grin. "No, you really hadn't gone that far under. I reached down and pulled you up out of the water from the side."

"But you're so wet."

He looked down and confirmed her diagnosis. "That was all water you brought up with you," he said cheerfully. "I guess I ought to get into some dry clothes, though. Could I borrow something of your husband's?''

''My husband's?'' She gazed at him blankly.

''Your husband's. I thought you had one of those.''

''Oh. Of course I do.'' She laughed shortly. ''Yes, just go down the hall to the bedroom on your right, next to the baby's room. There's a closet in there that should be full of stuff.''

He disappeared and she shivered, getting back under the spray, letting the delightful warmth spread throughout her body. And then she choked back a surge of hysteria. Good grief! She'd fallen into the pool and this incredibly handsome man had pulled her out and stripped her naked! Nothing quite this exciting had ever happened to her before and she was acting as though it were routine. And now he was going to be dressing in her husband's clothes. Her husband. What a laugh. It had been a while since she'd actually had one. But that was something no one else was to know about.

Craig had made a wonderful husband, at least in theory. Tall, handsome, distinguished looking, with credentials from the finest schools and most exclusive business firms, everyone had said they made a perfect couple when they got married.

Everyone, of course, didn't know what went on behind closed doors, which wasn't much as it turned out. But they had gotten along just fine for a few years. They were still good friends.

Though they had had their marriage annulled over a year ago, they hadn't told anyone. No one knew. Craig had agreed to that when Sara had asked for the favor. He knew her well enough to know how hard it would be for her to admit defeat to the world. And it meant nothing to him, really. Sometimes it was convenient to have a wife hanging around in the background.

He was in China on business at the moment, but he'd agreed to come home for the baby shower, to stand around and be her husband one more time, and she was grateful to him for that. This baby shower was going to be her showcase, her way of presenting herself and her life to all her old friends. She wanted everything to be just right, and that meant she really had to have a husband. Otherwise, it just wouldn't feel right.

Life had been too muddled lately. She needed a return to clarity. Having Craig here when she celebrated adopting the baby would help do that. Things would be back to normal. Almost.

Drey found the room and the closet, but the clothes weren't his style. He hesitated, then chose a polo shirt that was a size too small. His jeans were damp, but they would have to do. He couldn't see himself in the plaid slacks he found hanging among Sara's husband's things.

Walking out into the hallway, he listened. The water was still running. He turned toward the stairs and made his way down, searching until he found the den. Pulling out drawers in the desk, he uncovered an address book and quickly paged through it, calling the first doctor's name he could find there.

"Tell the doctor it's Sara Parker," he told the nurse who answered. "She's fallen into icy water and I think a doctor should take a look to make sure she's okay."

"Sara Parker?" The nurse sounded concerned. "Is this Mr. Parker?"

Drey caught back a smile. "No, it's not," he said, leaving the rest to the woman's imagination.

"I'm sure Dr. Bracken will want to stop by on his way home. Mrs. Parker is a close friend. He's leaving shortly and since he lives just a block away from Mrs. Parker..."

So that was settled. Drey hung up the telephone and sat for a moment, staring at the glass-enclosed bookshelves. Nice work. Everything in this house was first-class.

Even, he thought with a sudden grin, the woman.

She'd looked good in the pink cashmere suit and she'd looked even better without it. For a split second he allowed himself to think of her chilled skin, her long, molded legs, her round breasts, their nipples pulled into tight, dark buttons that made him...

No, he wasn't going to think that way. Quickly and resolutely, he shoved the picture of Sara's lovely naked body out of his mind. It wasn't fair to her to think about it and he wasn't going to do it.

Rising, he paced the room for a moment. What now? Every instinct in him told him to get out while the getting was good, to get as far away from this house and this woman as he could. But he hadn't completed the task he'd come for yet. His whole purpose in being here was to find out more about Sara Parker, to see what made her tick, to see what kind of a mother she was going to make for Jenny's baby. He was a long way from being able to make that sort of judgment. He couldn't leave for good until that determination was made.

Sara came down the stairs with a firm step. Her hair clung damply to her neck and there was still some part of her, deep inside, that was shaken by the accident. But she wasn't going to let that stop her. She had to find her helpful carpenter and face him right away, before the memory of what had just occurred, what he'd just done for her, started to eat into her self-confidence.

It took her breath away when she thought about it. There she'd been, stark naked in front of a strange and rather attractive man. What if he'd . . . ?

Well, it didn't help to think about what might have happened if he hadn't turned out to be a decent guy. Which he seemed to be. She was just lucky he'd been around to pull her out of the pool. Her nakedness was inconsequential compared to that.

But if she didn't find him, didn't talk about what had happened, laugh about it, she knew it would stay there inside her, like a worm in an apple and she couldn't let that happen.

She found him pacing the floor of her den and favored him with a bright smile meant to wipe away any nagging memories he might have of her unprotected body parts. "I want to thank you for what you did," she said, reaching out to take his hand in hers and gazing up at him earnestly.

He looked uncomfortable. "There's nothing to thank me for," he said gruffly.

There. She could see it in his eyes, in the set of his mouth. He was thinking about her naked. This was impossible, and if she didn't stop thinking about it herself, she was going to blush. She never blushed. She refused to blush. She had to get his mind on other things.

She hoped her laugh didn't sound as forced to his ears as it did to her own. "Are you kidding?" she said gaily. "You may have saved my life."

He looked startled to have her say such a thing. "I didn't save your life. You would have jumped out on your own in a few seconds."

"I'm not so sure about that," she told him. "Feel this."

She tossed her hair back and leaned her head to the side, guiding his hand to the area of her scalp where a huge goose egg was throbbing. It was strange to be inviting a perfect stranger to feel her head, but this was a strange situation, and he had probably saved her. That in itself was a fairly intimate act, wasn't it? And intimate acts tended to form bonds. *Consider one formed,* she told herself soothingly. *This man is now a close personal friend.*

"Ouch," he said, wincing for her as his fingers found the injury. "You hit your head, all right. You don't remember doing it?"

She shrugged. "I guess I missed it. There was a lot going on at the time." She shook her hair back and a slight frown formed between her brows. "I did feel like I was passing out at one point, though," she reflected.

He nodded, watching the way her hair fell into place in crisp waves. Damp like this, it still looked blond. Interesting. He supposed that meant it wasn't dyed but naturally light. The color of her eyebrows confirmed it. They were silky and light as the down on a peach.

She'd put on another sweater, this one a fuzzy soft baby blue. He glanced down. Sure enough, she'd put on baby blue socks to match. Concussion or not, she wasn't going to get sloppy. Maybe he was getting to know all about her after all.

"That's a nasty bump you've got," he told her with a direct look. "It's a good thing the doctor is on his way."

Her eyes widened. She hadn't wanted that. "What? You called the doctor?"

"Yes, I did."

She stared at him, resentful of his high-handed attitude. This carpenter she'd hired didn't seem to remember who the boss was. "I told you not to," she reminded him.

"Sorry about that." His dark eyes were coolly unrepentant and he went on, telling her the truth. "I very seldom do what I'm told."

She wasn't sure if she was angry or just amused. "What are you," she asked him bluntly. "Some sort of control freak?"

His mouth twisted into something that could almost be called a smile. "I like to call it being forceful and farsighted."

She was about to tell him what she called it when the doorbell chimed and she turned instead. "Oh drat, that will be the doctor."

"I'll get it," he said, starting for the door. "You sit down on the couch."

Outrage stiffened her back. It was pretty obvious this man was ready to take over everything if she let him. Cutting him off at the pass with an end run around the counter, she stood in his way, eyes narrowed.

"Excuse me," she said icily. "I believe this is my house. I'll get the door, thank you just the same."

He shrugged, unconcerned, looking down at her without rancor. "Are you sure you're okay?" he asked.

What was he trying to say, that he'd only been looking out for her welfare? She threw him a skeptical look and didn't bother to answer, striding quickly into the foyer with Drey right behind her.

She opened the door to find Dr. Bracken looking in anxiously, his huge gray eyes doleful as usual.

"Sara, my dear," he said, coming forward and taking her hand. "What happened?"

She smiled and glanced at Drey. "Nothing much, Matthew. I fell into the pool."

His kindly face registered extreme shock and alarm. "Oh, my God."

"No, don't get excited. There was water in it. Very cold water. And I bumped my head, which left a lump but not much else." She gave Drey a defiant look. "I didn't want you bothered with this. I'm perfectly fine."

"Well, that's to be determined, isn't it?" Dr. Bracken bustled in, shaking his head. "Come, my dear, you must sit down," he urged, leading her to a seat on a damask-covered chair in the parlor. "Let me take a look at you."

She did as he told her, displaying her goose egg bump one more time and submitting to the tiny light he shone into her eyes and to a reading of her heart rate. Matthew Bracken had been a friend and golfing partner of her ex-husband's ever since they'd moved to Denver three years before. Though she'd never taken him up on offers to get closer to his wife, she did like him.

"Craig still in China?" he asked as he studied her eyes.

"Yes," Sara replied.

"You know, I suddenly realized as I was driving over here that I haven't seen him for over a year. He and I used to get together for a game of golf about once a month, weather permitting, but it has been since the fall before last that we've played. How does the time get away from you like that?"

"Isn't that the truth?" Sara said evasively. "Maybe you can get him to play when he's here next week. We're having a lot of old friends from out of town to a baby shower and he promised to help me with it."

The doctor drew back and stared at her doubtfully. "So you're going through with this adoption scheme of yours?"

"Yes." She nodded, her eyes shining. "Yes, definitely."

He shook his head as though he didn't approve at all. "I don't know, Sara. I guess I said my piece when you called me a few months ago and asked my advice. I say there's no earthly reason you and Craig can't have a child of your own. You're both healthy and young enough. I've helped other couples, you know. There are ways. You never came in to see about—"

"Believe me, Matthew, we explored all the possibilities," she said hastily, glancing at Drey and hoping to stop the flow of the doctor's chatter. "We both decided. This is the best way. It's right for us."

"Well, that's neither here nor there," he muttered to himself as he began to put away his instruments. "You'll have to do what you think is right. But you'll need someone to watch you tonight. Better call in one of your friends."

Sara looked up at him, startled. "Why?"

He glanced at Drey. "Because I don't like the look of that knot on your head, and I'm not too sure about that pulse rate. It's up. I just want you watched, that's all. You might have a concussion." He hesitated. "Is there someone you can call? Someone who would come and stay with you?"

Sara shook her head slowly. She didn't even have to think it over. "There's no one. Matthew, you know I haven't made many women friends here in Denver. I've been too busy setting up the business."

"Oh, come now. There must be someone. Women always have friends all over the place."

Sara shook her head, dismissing the entire issue. She didn't want to bother Jenny, who had trouble getting around at this stage in her pregnancy. "I'll be fine. Don't worry."

The doctor frowned down at her. "But I do worry about you, Sara. Tell you what. I'll send Peggy, my wife, over. She'd be glad to—"

"No." Sara's voice had a note of final command. Having the sweet but talkative Peggy in her hair would drive her nuts. "I couldn't do that to your wife. Absolutely not."

"Now, Sara. Be reasonable. If not Peggy, there must be someone—"

"There's me."

They both turned and stared at Drey. Up to now, he'd been quietly standing in the background. The doctor had acknowledged his existence with a slight nod when he'd first come in, but other than that, he

might as well have been invisible. And now he was offering to stay.

Sara was speechless. This was the carpenter who'd
come to put up some shelves. It was all very well that
he'd pulled her out of a freezing pool, but that was no
reason he should move in with her. The man had
shown his high-handed attitude a few moments before. He had some nerve. But before she could bring
those considerations to light, the doctor spoke.

"Drey Angeli, isn't it?" Dr. Bracken said, squint-
ing at him. "You were a friend of my daughter Terry's, weren't you?"

Drey nodded. "That was a long time ago," he
noted. "Way back in high school."

"Ah yes. High school." The doctor gave a crunch-
ing laugh that shook his sturdy frame. "Terry was a
wild one in those days. She's settled down now, you
know. Got herself a degree in psychology and she's
giving tests to employees at one of the mining com-
panies. Lives in Aspen. Skis her heart out."

Drey's stern demeanor softened into a slight smile.
"Great. She always did love the snow."

"That she did." The doctor studied Drey for a moment, taking in his untamed hair and casual appearance, then glanced at Sara, his forehead scrunched in
a puzzled look. Suddenly his eyebrows rose as though
he'd realized something, and he cleared his throat.

"Well. Well now, okay, Sara. Drey is going to keep
his eye on you. That ought to do the trick. I guess I'll
stop by tomorrow and see how you're doing."

He started toward the foyer and Sara didn't budge.
She sat right where she was, watching him go and
wondering why she wasn't saying anything, why she

wasn't telling him Drey was not a friend, or whatever it was he assumed Drey was, that he was here to do a job and was not going to be staying. She knew she should tell him, that the situation cried out for her to say the words. But she also knew, if she told him that, it would start an argument. He would have Peggy over here in a flash. She decided to leave well enough alone and let him think what he wanted to think.

Drey noted Sara's reaction with amusement and took over, walking Dr. Bracken to the door and opening it for him. The doctor turned and nodded at him companionably, man to man.

"Look, I don't know what you're doing here," he said, leaning close. "And I don't ask questions. I do know Craig isn't the most attentive husband a woman could have. Still, people's lives are their own affairs. So to speak." He gave a quick cough of laughter. "But you treat that lady gently. She deserves it. And keep a look out for signs of seizure. You sometimes get that with a bad head trauma. You give me a call if anything worrisome shows up."

Drey nodded, leashing his smile. He didn't want to appear to take the doctor's words lightly. "I'll do that, sir. You can count on me."

"Good." He shook hands with the younger man. "I'll see you in the morning."

Drey watched him go, still suppressing a grin. The man thought he and Sara were lovers, and Sara had done nothing to disabuse him of that notion. Funny. He had no idea why she would let that theory fly, but he didn't much care, either. She had her own reasons, no doubt.

In the meantime, this was really a lucky break. It had fallen right into his lap. He was going to get an opportunity to see what Sara Parker was really like. And that was the whole reason he'd come.

Three

———

Drey retraced his steps into the parlor, but Sara was no longer sitting in the chair. Following the sounds of cabinets being opened, he found her in the kitchen, putting away clean dishes from the dishwasher. She barely glanced up at him as he entered the room.

"That's all a bunch of nonsense, of course," she said quickly. "I'm perfectly all right. You don't have to stay."

He slid onto a bar stool and leaned on the counter, watching her move. She had a glide to her movements, a grace that appealed to him. The image of her as a ballet dancer came to him again. She seemed to give the impression of being on her toes, even when her feet were flat on the ground.

"That's okay," he said smoothly. "I have nothing better to do."

Putting down the large pot she'd just pulled out of the washer, she turned to face him.

"Look," she said, her gaze frank and open. "I don't need you here. In fact, I really don't want you here. I have things to do and I want to be alone. When you come back in the morning—"

"I'm afraid I'm going to have to stay," he told her, breaking in with a certain arrogance. "I can't leave you alone after what happened."

She stared at him, trying to read what was going on in the depths of his smoky eyes. What exactly did he mean by that? What did he think had happened? Just because she'd fallen in the pool didn't mean she needed to be watched at all times. She wasn't likely to take a tumble into the hedgerow if he wasn't there to stop her.

Or was he talking about the nakedness? Did he think being with her in that state gave him some special right to her? If so, he might as well think again.

"I'm going to be perfectly frank with you here," she said at last. "You have done me a nice turn by saving my life, but when you come right down to it, I only met you today. I hardly know you. Why in the world would I let you stay overnight in my house?"

"Doctor's orders," he said as though that were his trump card.

She threw up her hands. "Oh, please. You know very well he assumed we were, well, something more than employer and employee."

"Yes, I know that." The grin he'd been hiding was finally getting too strong to hold back any longer and it shone in his dark eyes. "And you didn't do anything to correct that impression. Why not?"

She started to speak and then choked for a moment, color flooding her cheeks. Why not? That was a very good question. It was more than just not wanting Peggy as a roommate and she knew it. She just wasn't sure why.

"I...don't know," she said defensively. "The whole thing just caught me off guard."

That wasn't it and he knew it, too. He watched her, still wondering.

"The good doctor assured me he wasn't making judgments, but I would think you'd better correct the record at some point. Your husband might not be so understanding."

Her face seemed to change when he mentioned her husband, as though a cloud had come over her thoughts. "Never mind that," she said crisply. "I'll handle my reputation. In the meantime, the best way you can disprove the rumors would be to go. Right now."

She said it as though she expected him to jump up and run for the door, but he didn't move a muscle. Instead, he leaned back and looked at her through narrowed eyes.

"Well, this is your house," he said slowly, "and it is up to you. I'll go if you really want me to. But someone has to be here." A devilish light glittered in his eyes. "I can't in all conscience leave you without anyone. I'll have to call Dr. Bracken and let him know you're alone." He held back his amusement a moment longer. "I suppose he'll send his wife Peggy over and—"

She threw back her head, groaning and half laughing at the same time. "So, you play dirty, do you?" she accused him.

His grin was slow and his eyes were knowing, as though he could read her mind and knew he was going to be one step ahead of her. "If I have to."

"Well, I can play dirty, too," she declared, but when she tossed her head to emphasize her defiance, she set off a flash of pain that shot through her skull and the room swam before her. "Ouch," she said, closing her eyes and swaying against the counter.

Drey reacted without hesitation. "That does it," he said as he came down off the bar stool and stepped around the counter and took hold of her. "Come on. You're going to go lie down."

"No," she protested weakly. "No, I can't."

He swung her up into his arms without waiting to hear the rest of her speech and started for the stairs.

"I don't believe this," she murmured resentfully. "You can't just carry me around. I'm not a little girl."

"You're right," he said, taking the stairs easily. "You're a big, obstinate woman."

She wanted to fuss at him some more, but the pain in her head was disconcerting and her cheek felt so comfortable against his shoulder, she stayed quiet instead, closing her eyes and letting him take over. There was certainly an advantage in having a big strong man around. She felt protected and secure and that was nice—and so unusual for her.

When he gently laid her down on her bed, she almost regretted having to leave the warmth of his arms.

But he didn't seem to regret letting go. He backed away unceremoniously and glanced around the room.

"Do you have a radio in here?" he asked.

She looked up at him in surprise, shading her eyes from the light with her hand. "Yes. That's a clock radio on the bedside table."

"Good." He flicked it on and searched the stations until he found someone talking instead of music. "Listen to this," he advised. "Rest. You can even cover your eyes. But don't let yourself fall asleep."

"Okay," she said dutifully, feeling limp. "What are you going to be doing?"

"I'm going to fix us something to eat."

"You?" He didn't look like the sort of man who could be found adding basil to the vinaigrette, or even donning an apron and wielding a barbecue fork at the old gas grill. "You don't cook," she informed him skeptically.

"Don't I?" He favored her with a lopsided grin. "You just wait and see."

He left the room and she closed her eyes for a moment, resting her head, ignoring the voice on the radio and trying to think. She was actually very glad she was lying down, very glad Drey had taken over the way he had. He was right, and so was the doctor. She needed someone. The accident with the pool seemed to have sapped all her strength and had left her very shaken. She was grateful Drey wanted to stay. She would use this time to rest—and to think.

She'd been avoiding doing much thinking over the past few weeks. She'd been busy tying up the loose ends at her import company, fixing things so that she could take time off and get to know the new baby once it came. And she'd been frantically preparing for this baby shower she was having next week. All in all, thinking had been relegated to the sidelines. It was probably time to let it back into the game, at least for a few minutes.

It was odd how twisted her life had become lately. She'd had everything under control once. If she didn't watch out, things would fall apart and she would end up back where she'd been.

Her eyes popped open. Back where she'd been. Keeping away from that place was the driving force behind everything she did. She'd had a chaotic childhood. She would do everything she could to make sure she never went back there again.

On the outside, her life had probably looked idyllic. Her parents had plenty of money. What they didn't have was love, or any sense of what went into making a family. She still cringed remembering the late-night fights with people shrieking and racing through the house throwing things, her mother's boozy mornings, her father's affairs. As a little girl, she had hidden away from the pandemonium. She had a secret place in her closet with a little lamp and her special books, and she would go there and hide, making up a private world that the rest of her family knew nothing about. As an adult, she'd made that secret place her reality as much as she possibly could and for many years it seemed to work for her.

But little by little, things had begun to fall apart. First her marriage had become a sham, then it had evaporated completely. She'd tried hard to make it work and had built her business to take its place, but things just hadn't come together the way she needed them to. Then Jenny had told her about the pregnancy and she'd decided to adopt Jenny's baby. She knew she was taking a risk, but it was something she had to do. And she had to do it right.

"I'm in control," she muttered to herself. "Everything's going to be perfect."

Everything *was* going to be perfect. After all, she'd tamed the turmoil once before. She would do it again.

All you needed was a strong mind and you could set up your own reality. That was what it was all about.

But her reality was a little cockeyed at the moment. It would need some shoring up. First, instead of the perfect and ideal family she'd always thought she would have, she was about to be the single mother of her sister's child.

If that wasn't bizarre enough, she'd fallen into her pool and been rescued by her carpenter, who had stripped her naked without a second thought and was now downstairs fixing dinner.

Odd. Very odd. She was going to have to work to get things back on an even keel. And adopting Jenny's baby was going to be the first step, actually. It was a step she'd been working up to, a step she wanted very badly to take. If she couldn't have the perfect marriage, at least she would have the perfect baby.

When he left Sara in her bedroom, Drey started for the kitchen, but in the upper hallway he hesitated and instead turned toward the room where he'd found her husband's clothes. Something was nagging at him, something he hadn't been able to fit into the puzzle that was Sara.

Sara had told Dr. Bracken her husband was still on a trip to China, and the doctor seemed to accept that. There was really no reason Drey should question it. And, yet, something wasn't right.

He turned into the bedroom and looked at the neatly made bed, the dresser with its picture of Sara and its neatly placed, silver-backed brush-and-comb set. There was a static quality to the room, as though it were a set for a play, not a place where real people lived. He wasn't sure why, but something felt wrong.

"In the first place, what kind of a husband sleeps in a separate room?" he muttered to himself, about to open the closet. A quick mental image of Sara's sleek, naked body flashed into his mind and he bit down hard on his lip to force it away. He wasn't going to let himself think of her as a desirable woman, no matter how good she looked with her clothes off. That wasn't what he was here for.

But it did bring up the question—how could a man who loved her stay away?

Each to his own way of living. Wasn't that the sort of toleration everyone was supposed to practice these days?

Sure, but not where a baby was involved. He'd made a commitment to make sure Jenny's baby was going to a good home. So far, he wasn't sure that was what he would call this one.

He turned to the closet and pulled it open, still searching for the element that had bothered him when he'd been here before. Rows of suits hung side by side with polo shirts and winter jackets. He stared at them and the answer came to him. These things hadn't been touched in months, possibly years. The suits were out of style. The jackets looked like castoffs. And the entire collection had the odd, musty smell of fabric in storage. If Sara's husband ever came home, he didn't come here.

Drey closed the closet door and turned slowly, heading for the kitchen once again. He'd learned long ago that things were seldom as they seemed on the surface, but this was extreme. Where was Sara's husband? Or did she even have one?

It was not merely an interesting question. It was something he had to know.

* * *

"Hey, no sleeping."

Sara opened her eyes. She had drifted off for just a moment, but she was awake now, and there Drey was, looking down at her. She frowned.

"Why are you doing this?" she asked him.

"To keep you awake. I'm just checking on you. It's not good for someone with a possible concussion to go to sleep right away."

"No, that's not what I mean." She turned and punched the pillow up, then half sat against it. "Why are you helping me this way?"

"I have nothing better to do," he claimed, but there was a veiled look in his eyes and she didn't believe him.

There was another reason. She was not so naive as to think he was doing this out of the goodness of his heart.

Should she be frightened of him? She asked herself that as he left the room again, going down to finish cooking. He was a stranger and he was staying the night. Was she crazy to let him? Was she nuts?

Probably. But she knew the man he worked for. And Matthew Bracken said he'd been friends with his daughter in high school. That made him about five years younger than she was, but it also made him someone people in her circle knew. Was all this enough to guarantee he was a good guy?

She still didn't have her answers, but she resigned herself to being taken care of. It felt so darn good. No one had taken care of her this way since... She thought hard, but she couldn't remember when anyone else had done it. From the time she was a child she'd always been taking care of other people, trying to make everything work and holding it all together.

That was what was wrong. Things weren't holding together anymore. Everything seemed to be flying apart. But she didn't want to think about that.

Closing her eyes, she tried to listen to what the man was saying on the radio, but he was talking politics and she wasn't tuned in to that channel at the moment. Disobeying direct orders, she dozed.

She hated to admit it, but he was a darn good cook. Cheese omelets, chicken broth and garlic bread. Not the most conventional dinner, but very tasty.

They sat facing each other at the little table in the breakfast nook. She couldn't eat more than a few bites of everything, but those few bites were great, and she told him so.

"I'm impressed," she told him. "I thought you would open a can or thaw something from the freezer."

"I could have done that," he admitted. "But I knew that wouldn't come up to your standards."

"My standards." She savored the concept. Most people seemed to think *standards* was a dirty word. "What do you know about my standards?"

He shrugged. "I can take a look around this house and see that you like things done right."

He'd noticed. That pleased her and she smiled as she took another bite of his golden omelet. "Would you like some wine?" she asked, suddenly thinking of it.

He hesitated. "You shouldn't drink any," he reminded her.

"I know. But *you* didn't get hit in the head." She rose and opened the refrigerator, taking out a long, slender bottle and grabbing a wineglass off the shelf. "You can have a sip or two."

She poured it out for him, golden liquid catching the light and shimmering in the crystal glass, echoing the sense of spun gold her hair had now that it had dried and was flying around her face like a cloud. He liked the way she looked, liked the way it felt to watch her. Something about her standing there, so pretty, pouring him wine, did something to him, sent a warmth into his blood. He only let himself enjoy it for a moment, then pushed it away. No traps. He knew how to avoid them.

He finished eating quickly and leaned back in his chair, watching her pick at her food. She wasn't hungry, that was clear, but he didn't suppose it meant anything. She was very slender and she probably wasn't hungry much of the time. He glanced at her hands, noting the wrists that looked as fragile as glass. These were the hands that were going to be caring for Jenny's baby very soon.

"Tell me about this baby you're adopting," he asked her, trying to sound casual.

She looked up, wondering at the question. He wasn't the sort for idle conversation. "What do you want to know?" she asked, suddenly suspicious.

He shook his head, avoiding her eyes for the moment. "The usual questions. Why, when, where, who and how."

A frown marred her pretty face. "Too vague," she said primly.

He turned his attention on her again. "Okay, how's this?" he asked, his eyes narrowed and his gaze watchful, as though he didn't want to miss any clues she might throw out. "Is your husband as excited about this adoption as you are?"

Her husband. She turned away. No one knew about the annulment. No one knew that she and Craig were no longer a real couple. And that was the way she wanted it.

It had been eighteen months since Craig had left. As an international banker, he had often taken trips overseas before. Now, whenever anyone asked, she said he was on a business trip, and so far, no one had questioned it.

Luckily there weren't many who might have. She and Craig had lived in Denver for three years, but they had few friends. She'd been involved in setting up her import business and he'd been away on business trips. People were used to him being gone. It seemed natural.

"Craig... Craig isn't here much," she said, following the usual line. "He won't really be involved in raising the baby like I will."

"Is that right?" He leaned forward as though he'd won a concession from her. "Don't you think it's important for kids to have the influence of a father in their lives?"

She raised her silver blue gaze and stared into his opaque eyes. Why on earth did this man think this was any of his business?

"What about you?" she asked him deliberately. "Are you married? Do you have any children?"

"No on both counts."

She smiled, feeling just a bit triumphant. "Then you don't know anything about babies, either."

He hesitated. This wasn't about him, it was about her. But then, she didn't know that and he supposed he ought to make an effort at normal conversation if he wanted this to get anywhere.

"That's not really true," he told her reluctantly. "I grew up in a family full of kids and I've taken care of babies all my life."

"Oh." Her smile drooped and she raised one eyebrow, annoyed at him. Why did he seem so contradictory all the time?

"Who's going to take care of this baby when it comes?" he asked, not letting it go.

She took a deep breath and glared at him. "I am. I'm going to be the mother, remember?"

"But if you don't know anything about it..."

Good grief, the man was a pest. Why did he care, anyway? "I've hired a nurse," she said shortly. *So there.*

His mouth twisted and not with humor. This was just what he'd been afraid of. "Is that the way you take care of all life's little troubles? Hire an expert to handle them for you?"

She drummed her fingertips on the table to keep from reaching for a plate to throw at his head. "Wait a minute. First you complain that I don't know how to take care of a baby, then you complain that I've hired someone to help me. You can't have it both ways."

"Sure I can." He said it with that male smugness that made her want to scream.

"No, you can't. It's not fair." She would have tossed her head if she hadn't been afraid to start the headache up again. "Anyway, I took some child-care classes at the hospital, which is more than most first-time mothers do. I'll be up to speed in no time.''

"No doubt.'' The words dripped with sarcasm.

She threw him one last glare and rose, piling dishes together. "Never mind,'' she said coolly. "The shelves will be built and you'll be gone long before that baby gets here. So it won't be any concern of yours, will it?''

He let that one fly on past. Instead of answering, he followed her, bringing along the rest of the dishes and putting a stack in the sink. She rinsed them and began filling the dishwasher while he leaned against the counter, watching her.

"You feeling okay?'' he asked softly.

She turned and nodded, and at the same time her anger melted away. There was real concern in his dark eyes. This was the man who'd pulled her out of the pool and taken care of her ever since. Now he was showing concern for her child. What was there to get angry about?

A wave of remorse washed over her and she reached out and took his hand, gazing up into his face with quick affection and gratitude.

"I want to thank you, Drey,'' she said. "You've been great. I don't know how to express to you how grateful I am.''

He stared down at her for a moment, looking unconvinced. "Give it up,'' he advised serenely. "I'm not going to leave. I'm staying for the night and you might as well get used to it.''

She dropped his hand and frowned at him again. He couldn't even take a compliment without looking for an ulterior motive.

"I wasn't going to tell you to go,'' she said, although that was fudging the truth a little.

Actually she still had that in mind. There was really no reason for him to stay. She had a bump on her head and that was all. She was fine. And he was still just the carpenter. It seemed too odd to have him stay the night with her.

"Weren't you?" He slid back onto the bar stool and gazed at her, his eyes reflecting his cynical mood.

She stared back at him, truly mystified. What was the man's reason for wanting to stay? She could have understood it if he'd had a little romance in mind, or maybe the hope that the rich lady would fork over more money. But the longer she knew him, the more she was sure neither motive belonged to him at all.

She leaned on the other side of the counter and tried to figure him out. He wasn't like the men she usually dealt with. He didn't have the polished manners or the superior attitude. But there was something strong about him, strong and basic, and she decided there was a part of her that sort of liked it. And another part that considered him high-handed and primitive and didn't like it at all.

She couldn't help but notice that the polo shirt he'd taken from Craig's closet fit him a lot more snugly than it had ever fit her ex-husband. There was a solid chest there and some outrageously huge muscles nicely outlined by the taut fabric. Some women would have considered him sexy. Not her, of course, but some women . . .

He was speaking again and she looked up at his face with a guilty start.

"Listen, Sara Parker," he was saying softly, his gaze intense. "I want you to tell me the truth about something."

She blinked at him, all innocence. Why would she lie? "What about?"

His dark eyes seemed to glitter in the kitchen light. "Why isn't your husband around? The real story."

He caught her unguarded and her gaze wavered. "What are you talking about? I've told you that already. He's...he's on a trip to China. He's coming back next week."

He shook his head slowly, not buying it. "Nice try, but it just won't wash. I've been in his room and I've seen his things. The last time he was in that room, Eisenhower was still president."

Now she was feeling attacked. What gave him the right to ask her these things? "I hardly think so," she snapped back, eyes flashing. "I wasn't even born when Eisenhower was president."

He waved her retort away. "You're ducking the question." His gaze hardened along with the line of his mouth. "Tell the truth. Does this husband of yours really exist?"

This was the first time she'd really been challenged on this issue and she wasn't prepared like she should have been. She hadn't expected the emotional impact to hit her this way. No husband. She had no husband. This was not good and it shook her. And yet, she couldn't just collapse in a heap on the floor. She had to fight back.

Though she still couldn't meet his gaze, her chin jutted out. "You know, I don't see what gives you the right—"

His hand reached out like the strike of a snake and grabbed her wrist. "More evasions," he said firmly. "Look me in the eye and tell me the truth."

She winced, trying to look into his eyes and faltering. "Why? What does it matter to you, anyway?"

His fingers held her wrist loosely, but he didn't let go. "That's not the point," he said, using some evasion of his own. "Your husband is the point."

"My husband is none of your business," she said, her irritation with this line of questioning reaching meltdown. "What do you care where he is?"

He hesitated. This was getting him nowhere. He couldn't very well browbeat information out of her. It might be wise to lose the stern, overbearing act and be a little more natural. After all, most people considered him a friendly guy. Why was he treating her as though she might pick his pocket if he didn't pay attention?

He knew the answer to that one, though he resisted facing it. He was finding her too damn attractive. The ice had melted and revealed a warm-blooded woman. And besides—he couldn't get the picture of her naked body out of his head.

There. He'd admitted it. So it did all boil down to the old libido, no matter how high-and-mighty he might pretend to be. What a jerk he was.

Obviously it was time to reform his ways and shift his tactics. When he met her eyes again, he let the hint of a coaxing smile show in his face.

"It's only natural that I'd want to know something about your husband," he reminded her. "If he were to walk in right now, what would he think?"

"Of you being here?" There had been a time when she'd considered having an affair, just to see if it were possible to make Craig jealous. But she'd never had the nerve to go through with it. And she knew now that it would have made no difference to him. She shrugged. "Not a thing. So forget about him."

How could he? He was beginning to get very suspicious about the man. Did he exist?

"I like to get the groundwork in when I sleep over," he said lightly. "I want to know what to expect. I want to know whether I should be prepared to jump out a window if we hear a car in the driveway."

She wasn't mollified. "Don't be ridiculous."

His eyes were hinting at humor. "I don't know. Is he the jealous type? What do you usually do with your lovers when he comes home unexpectedly?"

She stared at him, openmouthed, then yanked her hand away from his. "I think you should go," she said fiercely.

He shook his head. He shouldn't have said that. He knew he'd insulted her, and though he hadn't really meant to do it, she had a right to take it that way. Still, he wasn't going to back down. He couldn't. Not yet.

"I don't think so," he responded, as casual as ever. "I think I'll stay. Maybe this husband will show up."

"Maybe," she snapped. "But you'll be gone if he does."

She glared at him across the countertop and he held her gaze without flinching. Slowly he shook his head again.

"Sara, you're about to adopt a baby," he said in a reasonable voice. "You have no husband around. I just think it would be a good idea if you analyzed the situation before you jump into it. I'm wondering what sort of life you are preparing for this baby. What exactly do you think you're doing here?" He could see by the softening of her face that he was getting to her and that was a relief. He wanted to be sure she understood what she was getting into. He'd been afraid from the first that this might be just a rich woman's whim.

"A baby isn't a doll," he added softly. "It isn't a puppy you can stick in a kennel when you want it out of the way."

She pushed her hair back with a nervous hand. "I know that."

He watched her for a moment, then went on. "I'm not sure you know it. You say you don't know anything about raising children and I believe it. Raising a baby is a serious undertaking. It's an eighteen-year commitment. You don't do something like that on an impulse."

She looked at him again. What was he, the voice of her conscience? These were the same questions and accusations she'd been pushing aside in her mind for weeks. She had been putting off dealing with them, but the time had come.

And now here was this man, voicing the very concerns she'd had and hadn't resolved. The coincidence was eerie. She stared at him, looking hard.

"Where did you come from?" she asked him, wondering. "What are you doing here?"

He gave a grunt of impatience. "I'm the carpenter, remember? I came to build some shelves."

Of course. That was all he was. Mentally she shook herself and got back on track. "And stayed to run my life for me?" she responded tartly.

He shrugged. "I'm only trying to get you to face reality."

Reality. What did he know about it? A sudden anger filled her, crashed through her and she blurted, "All right. You want the truth? Here's the truth. Craig and I haven't been married for a year and a half."

There. She'd said it. She hadn't told another living soul, and she'd just spilled the whole story to a carpenter she'd only met hours before. She looked around, almost fearing she might be struck dead for her sins. But nothing happened. The sky didn't fall. The earth didn't split. And Drey didn't gasp.

In fact, he took it awfully calmly, nodding as though he'd known it all along.

"No husband," he said softly, his mouth set in a grim line. That was exactly what he'd been afraid of.

Oh, Jenny, Jenny, he said silently, shaking his head. There were a thousand nice and stable couples who were on waiting lists all over Colorado, dying for a child of their own. And Jenny was letting her unmarried sister raise her baby.

This was just what he'd come here to find out. And now that he knew, what was he going to do with the information? He'd thought it would be easy, but now that he was getting to know Sara, it was getting complicated all over again. He could see fleeting evidence of the pain in her eyes. He could see the longing. If he put a stop to this adoption, it was going to hurt her. But he had to think of the child first.

"No husband," he said again, shaking his head.

She nodded, feeling dispirited. "That's right," she said bleakly. "I have no husband."

"Any prospects in the offing?" His cool gaze examined her as though he were evaluating her chances on the marriage market. "Are you romantically involved with anyone?"

"No." She took a deep breath, forcing herself to regain some spirit. Gathering her resources, she gazed at him defiantly. "Actually, I'm not really the romantic type," she told him smoothly.

"Aren't you?"

"No. I'm the practical type."

He stared at her for a long moment, while she watched his eyes, and then his grin surfaced. "You could have fooled me," he said softly, and suddenly the two of them were laughing together.

"I know, I know. It's crazy," she told him, feeling as though a weight had lifted from her shoulders. Laughter was better than wine at getting people closer. "The whole situation is insane. But...there's more to this than you know about. I really can't go into the background, the reasons." She stared at him, her clear gaze earnest. "All I can tell you is, I'm going to do the best job I can raising this baby. I'm going to work harder at this than I've worked on anything in my life."

He believed her. That was what made it all so difficult. He could see the determination in her, see what she did with her life around here. She went after things, and she would go after this. The only problem was, would it be enough? A baby's future was at stake.

The air between them seemed to have cleared now that the secret she'd been hiding was out in the open. She could laugh and he could smile and they could hold a conversation without veiled accusations and stormy denials. And they could talk about the baby.

They went into the living room and sat on the floor at the coffee table while she showed him things in the stack of catalogs of baby furniture and baby clothes she'd accumulated over the past few weeks. They talked softly for another hour, talked about babies and snow and whether Denver was better than California, and he watched her eyes and the way she threw back her head when she laughed and he realized he liked her. The stories Jenny had told him didn't hold water. Sara was a perfectionist, but she was no ice princess. There was passion in her, warmth, all the qualities that went into being a good mother.

But she was an unmarried woman and he wasn't sure yet what he was going to do about that. Still he had time. Jenny was due to deliver on Sunday. And plenty of babies were overdue. He had a few days to think things over.

"I'm fine, you know," she said at last. "My headache is even gone. I think you could go home and sleep in your own bed."

He stretched his long legs out and leaned back, gazing at her from beneath lowered eyelids. "One thing you'll learn about me, Sara Parker," he said drowsily. "I finish what I start. I am not a quitter."

She laughed softly. "I guess that means you're here for the night, doesn't it?"

He nodded. "For the duration," he added.

She sighed. "All right then. You can sleep in Craig's room. The bed should be made up. I had it ready for next week."

He nodded, then looked at his watch and began adjusting the dials. "I'll wake you up at three," he warned her. "Just to check."

"You'll do no such thing. I want to sleep." She rose and turned and went light-headed all at the same time, losing her balance and lurching back toward the floor. He caught her before she landed, swearing softly as he pulled her up into his arms.

"Yeah, you're doing fine," he said sarcastically. "Never better, huh?"

"I just got up too fast," she protested, but she didn't struggle out of his arms and, after looking down

at her and studying her eyes, he was satisfied that she
was probably right. Still he didn't want to let her go,
and he began carrying her toward the stairs.

"I can walk," she said, but not very insistently.

"I'm sure you can," he responded. "But I can carry
you."

She sighed, luxuriating in the protective attention.
"We can't keep meeting like this," she murmured.

"Why not?"

Smiling, she snuggled against his shoulder. He was
so hard and he smelled of wine and maleness and the
sense of him swept over her, catching at her breath.
She could close her eyes and dream he was her lover
and she was tempted. It had been so long since any
man had been this close to her. It had been forever
since she'd felt desire stir inside her. Maybe that was
why it threatened to send her into a tailspin right now.

"You smell good," she told him sleepily.

"So do you," he responded, his arms tightening
around her just a bit.

Whoa, he told himself silently at the same time. He
could feel the way she was nestling against him, and to
him that signaled an acceptance he hadn't asked for,
didn't want. He wasn't here to play games.

He laid her back on her bed, settling her among her
fluffy covers, and as he drew away, his hand acciden-
tally brushed her breast. She gazed up at him, her
heart beating wildly as he paused above her.

He could see the sudden awareness in her eyes and
he knew it probably wouldn't take much to get her to
welcome him into her bed. A picture of her slick, naked body flashed into his mind again, together with
the imprint of her soft breast along the back of his

hand, and his own body reacted. She would be sweet to make love to, sweet and rich and...

He drew back, shocked at his own thoughts. He couldn't make love with Sara. Not ever. She was Jenny's sister.

"I'll look in on you at three," he repeated gruffly, turning away, and then he was gone.

Sara lay very still. She could still feel where his hand had touched her breast so lightly. She could still feel the sense of shelter she'd had in the strength of his arms.

"I can still respond to a man," she whispered to herself. "What do you know?"

Four

——

Sara woke up at five of three and stared at the clock, listening. It wasn't long before she heard Drey coming down the hall. True to his promise—but somehow she'd known he would be. He opened the door to her room. The light from the hallway flooded in on her.

She sat up, clutching the covers to her chest, put one hand to her eyes to cut the glare and smiled at him.

"Hi," she said brightly.

He went still in the doorway.

"You're already awake," he said as though that were a problem.

"Yes." She squinted, looking at him beyond the light. He was barefoot and wearing nothing but the bottoms of an old pair of Craig's pajamas. He looked huge and shaggy, like a dream she might have had. "I've been waiting for you," she told him, and that seemed dreamlike, too.

He sighed and dropped to sit on the side of her bed, switching on the lamp at her bedside. "You see, the whole point was to see how easy it was for you to wake up from a sound sleep," he explained.

"Obviously it was pretty darn easy," she observed, trying not to notice how hard the rounded muscles of his chest looked in the golden light. His naked torso was only inches away and it looked like marble lovingly sculpted, like something beyond real flesh and blood. He looked as though he would be hot to touch and she wished she had the nerve to reach out and see if he was. But he was too beautiful in the lamplight. He was so gorgeous it was scary, and her heartbeat began a steady acceleration.

If he was feeling any of the same sensual vibrations in the air, he wasn't letting on. "How do I know for sure you've been asleep at all?" he asked suspiciously, all business.

She ventured a tremulous smile. "You'll have to trust me on that one."

He grunted and tilted the lampshade to get more light. "Hold still. Let me look into your eyes."

She tried not to blink while he studied her pupils, but he was so close and the light was glaring and she finally winced away, dropping the covers at the same time.

"I'm fine, you know," she insisted, groping to pull the covers back.

"That's an understatement," he muttered under his breath as his gaze slid over the way she looked in her lacy blue nightgown. It wasn't really meant for her to hear, but she did, and she flushed and hurried to cover her breasts.

It was funny, she thought, how his seeing her completely naked earlier in the evening hadn't really bothered her at all, but his now noticing the way the lace only barely concealed her breasts with their tight, dark nipples seemed impossibly provocative.

"Okay," he said, getting up abruptly as though he'd been struck by the same paradox. "I guess we'd better get back to sleep."

He went toward the doorway and she watched, amazed at how beautiful his body was, like one of those statues of a classical athlete holding a discus or straining to lift a heavy weight.

"Good night," he said, looking back.

"Good night," she echoed softly, wishing he wasn't leaving.

But the door closed and his steps retreated down the hall and she slowly sank back into her comforter.

"The morning will bring sanity," she promised herself. "You'll forget all about having a crush on the carpenter."

But at the moment it was the middle of the night and her eyes stayed open for a long time. Sanity seemed very far away.

Drey lay back in his bed and stared into the darkness, listening to the wind whistle around the eaves of the house. He'd slept in strange houses before, stayed overnight with women he hardly knew. But this was probably the oddest instance of it he'd ever experienced. Now here he was, trying to picture what Sara would be like as the mother to Jenny's baby, and another picture kept getting in the way—a picture of what Sara would be like lying here beside him in this cold, lonely bed.

He should have skipped the three-o'clock visit. Seeing her like that, her hair all loose around her shoulders, her eyes luminous in the lamplight, her nightgown sheer and skimpy, he'd been hit by a wave of urgent desire like he hadn't felt since he was seventeen. Teenage hormones. That was what he was being plagued with. And that wasn't what he'd come here for.

He'd come to check out Sara Parker as soon as he'd found out she was adopting Jenny's baby. He'd been worried. Knowing Jenny the way he did, he hadn't expected much.

It wasn't that he hadn't liked Jenny. For the short period of time they'd dated, they'd had a lot of fun together. They'd done some crazy things and he'd never considered her wife material—for him or for anyone else, for that matter. She was still a little too young, a little too careless. So when he'd heard about the baby, he'd been concerned. He'd felt it was his duty to look into the arrangements Jenny had made, make sure she was doing the right thing. And when he'd heard she was giving the baby up for her sister to adopt, he'd groaned. He'd known he would have to look into it, make sure she wasn't doing something completely off-the-wall.

But Sara had surprised him. She wasn't a bit like her sister, and she wasn't a bit like the ogre Jenny had painted her when they'd dated. She would probably make a pretty good mother for any child, if she could get over this obsession with appearances and play life straight. Still the situation wasn't quite right. He was a firm believer in a child being raised with two parents whenever possible, and that wasn't what was going to happen here.

When he'd first heard from a slip Jenny's friend Rachel made that Jenny was pregnant, he'd tried to call her, knowing from the dates that the baby was probably his. She wouldn't take his calls, didn't return them, disappeared when he came around. But he'd finally tracked her down, and she confirmed his fears—and told him she was planning to give the baby up for adoption. He'd agonized for a while. After all, the baby was as much his responsibility as it was Jenny's. Maybe he should take the little tyke himself.

But what the hell was he going to do with a baby? Unless he married somebody quickly, the child wouldn't have a mother. No, he couldn't take it. Still, he knew he owed it more than casual notice. He'd decided it was up to him to make sure that baby went to a good home. Was that what Sara was going to provide? That was what he aimed to find out.

Anyway, he wasn't really worried about the attraction he was feeling toward Sara, no matter how strong and sly it was. After dating Jenny, he'd sworn off women. He'd decided to concentrate on strengthening his own building design business instead of wasting time and effort in a constant search for the good life.

"Good idea," his mother had said firmly. "You've had enough party time in your young lifetime to last for the rest of your days. It's about time you got serious."

He'd taken her advice to heart and he'd worked hard. His business was thriving. But lately his brother Rick had begun to meddle in his plans, contradicting his mother and undermining his serious tone.

"All work and no play means you're getting to be boring as hell," he'd quipped the other morning over coffee and doughnuts. "You need a little dose of female companionship. If you don't do something soon, you're going to forget how it's done."

Drey had made a face. "I hardly think so," he'd responded dryly.

"Come on, little brother," Rick had cajoled, waving a jelly-filled cruller at him. "You've got to have a woman in your life. Tell you what. You need a wife."

Drey had thrown him a disbelieving look. "Why?"

Rick shook his handsome head. Tall and blond, he looked like a surfer gone straight. He was happily married with three little girls and a career as an accountant with a large firm. All he really wanted was for his brother to be as happy as he was.

"You need someone to cook your food and support you when you're down and iron your shirts. And most of all—" he gave him a lascivious wink "—to warm your bed at night."

Drey put down his coffee cup and looked almost as cynical as he felt. "Sounds good. If that was all there was to it, I'd run down to the wife store and pick up one tonight and get her started." He leaned back on the two rear feet of his chair and grinned at his brother. "But I've been around the block, O older and wiser brother, and I happen to know that most models come equipped with a few other features that aren't so adorable."

Rick looked blank. "Like what, for instance?"

"Like a life plan for molding men." He let the chair back down with a sharp thump. "I guarantee you a wife would be after me to cut my hair, get rid of my motorcycle and wear a tie to work before the rice had fallen out of her ears."

Rick laughed and shook his head. It was pretty obvious he had no real defense to that. "Aren't you aching to hear the patter of little feet?" he asked, instead of pursuing it.

Drey shrugged. "Sure. But only if those little feet belong to a German shepherd or a nice collie."

Rick threw back his head and groaned. "Drey, baby, you don't know what you're missing. Every man should have a wife. That's what life is all about."

Drey took a last sip of coffee and shoved the cup away. "Let me get this straight. Aren't you here sleeping on my couch because Mary kicked you out last night?"

Rick shrugged, looking shifty. "Sure."

"Wasn't there something about spending your entire paycheck on a new set of golf clubs?"

"Yeah." Rick settled back in his chair, seemingly totally at peace with himself and his situation. "But in a few hours the phone will ring and she'll be crying and saying she's sorry and wants me back." He smiled smugly. "And I'll go home and we'll make up. And..." He gave his brother a significant look. "Listen, Drey. Making up is nice to do." He sighed happily, his eyes dreamy. "And that, my friend, is the happy ending. That's what it's all about."

Drey shook his head, not tempted in any way by his brother's vision of life as he knew it. "Between playing golf and making up with Mary, you've got your entire life planned, don't you?" Drey rose and took his cup to the sink, ready to change the subject.

"You don't know what you're missing," Rick insisted. "Tell you what. I'm going to find you a girl."

Drey uttered an ugly curse and turned to stomp out of the room, but his brother called after him. "I'm going to set you up with that cute new girl in finance. Some French name. Gigi or Gogo or something like that. She'll turn you around. One look and you'll be hooked.''

Another curse came flying back at Rick, but he grinned and nodded. "Yup," he said softly to himself. "Drey needs a woman, and I'm going to make sure he gets one."

Rick wasn't any more a quitter than Drey was, and by the next day, he'd coerced him into agreeing to a blind date with the allegedly lovely Gigi. Drey winced, remembering. If he had his calendar marked right, the date was supposed to be on the night coming up. He was going to have to remember to call her and cancel. Lying in the bed in Sara's spare room, he regretted having agreed to it more than ever. A good excuse was all he needed.

Turning on his side, he closed his eyes, and in no time, he was asleep.

Suddenly it was morning. Sara felt better and the lump on her head had gone down considerably. Dressed in a cream-colored jumper, makeup already carefully applied, she went down to the kitchen and started the coffee.

She'd spent the past few hours dreaming about muscular men playing volleyball on a beach where the sand kept turning into hot coals every time she tried to step out on it.

"Something is telling me to stay away from muscular men," she told herself sternly as she filled the coffeepot with water. "Wise advice. I'll try to follow it to the letter."

But sanity still seemed elusive. She couldn't stop thinking about how Drey had looked during the night and she knew she was waiting with bated breath for him to show up.

She planned to be cool. She planned to be calm, and maybe even slightly superior, just to let him know there was nothing going on here. At least, nothing that might be construed as physical attraction.

After all, she tried to remind herself, she was at least five years older than he was. And she was a little busy here. She was about to adopt a baby. She was about to have a party for all her old friends so that they could see how perfectly happy she was. This was the way she'd planned it and she couldn't do anything to throw her life off track.

She certainly wasn't in the market for a quick and exciting affair—though that thought did make her heart beat faster. When she thought of the way he'd looked the night before, the way his hand had felt on her breast, the way his gaze had felt—but no, that was just the point. She wasn't going to think about those things at all.

But she heard him coming down the stairs and she knew it was going to be hard not to. What was she going to do to stop it?

"Sing," she told herself urgently, pressing down the button on the coffee grinder and grinding as hard as she could. "Sing something. Anything."

The song "Crazy" came to mind and she began humming it to the rhythmic pulse of the coffee grinder.

"You sound cheerful this morning," he said behind her, and she stopped grinding, putting down the little machine carefully and taking a deep breath before she turned. If he'd come down with his shirt off...

But no. As she turned, she saw with a mixture of relief and disappointment that he'd dressed in his jeans and shirt from the day before. His buckskin jacket was slung over his shoulder. He looked entirely presentable, though his dark eyes were just as smoky as they'd been the night before, and his full, sensual lips seemed to draw her gaze like a magnet.

"Where are you going?" she asked quickly.

"Home," he replied. "I need to shave and wash up."

The night's worth of beard was incredibly attractive and she began to feel the need to sing again. "Wouldn't you like a cup of coffee and something to eat before you go?"

He shook his head. "Thanks, but I'd better get going. I'll be back this afternoon to get going on those shelves."

Stepping closer, he reached out and tilted up her face with a finger under her chin. "How are you doing this morning?" he asked, examining her eyes.

"I'm...a lot better," she mumbled, swallowing hard.

He nodded, and before she realized his intention, he had a hand in her hair, feeling for the bump. "Swelling's gone down," he murmured, touching gently with probing fingers.

He dropped his gaze and met hers and something cracked between them, something that stung and cried out for notice. His hand cupped the back of her head as though he were considering pulling her to him, and his attention went to her mouth.

She held her breath, sure he was about to kiss her. She didn't bother to think about singing any longer.

This had gone beyond any help singing could give her. He was going to kiss her and she could hardly wait.

And then the telephone rang. It rang out loud and clear and they both jumped a foot, as though they'd suddenly been grabbed from behind and forced back into the real world from some sort of foggy fantasy.

He dropped his hand and drew back and she turned blindly toward where the phone was screeching, the sound annoyingly horrible to her senses.

"Yes?" she said breathlessly as she put the receiver to her ear.

"Sara?" The voice was that of Jenny. "Sara, is that you?"

"Yes, Jenny," Sara said, settling herself as best she could. "What is it?"

"Oh, nothing. I just thought you'd like to know. I had your baby last night."

Sara caught her breath, stunned. "You . . . you what?"

"Had the baby. Calli is her name. You'd better come and get her."

For some reason, Sara's brain refused to accept it. "But that can't be. You're not due until—"

"Tell that to the baby, sister dear. She's here. And she's definitely not going back where she came from until a more convenient time for us all."

Realization was finally sinking in and Sara was trembling. "Why didn't you call me?" she wailed. "I could have been with you."

"No problem. I had Jake with me."

"Jake?" She clutched the receiver. "Who's Jake?"

"The guy I'm going to Florida with when I get out of here. Will you come on down so we can get the paperwork over with?"

"I . . . I'll be there right away." She started to hang up, then remembered and jammed the receiver back against her ear. "Wait! Jenny, how are you?"

"I'm fine. The delivery was a cinch. I was only in real labor for two hours. The baby is perfect. Seven pounds four ounces, nineteen inches long. I saw her for a minute and she's gorgeous. So come take care of her already."

"I'm coming," Sara said, and this time she managed to let go of the connection. Turning, she stared blindly at Drey. "The baby is here," she said, shaking her head. "I can't believe it."

Drey watched her, watched what was going on in her eyes. He'd overheard the conversation and had studied her as it went on and he knew what was happening. She was scared to death now that this was really coming true. And to make matters worse, so was he.

"Okay, I've got to be calm," she was saying, wringing her hands. "Let's see. First things first." She gazed at him, her eyes wide with question. "But what was first?" she wailed. "Oh, I know!" she added before he had a chance to respond. "The nurse. I've got to call the nurse I hired." She reached for the receiver again.

He stopped her with a hand over the telephone. "Never mind getting in touch with the nurse just yet," he said. "I'll help you."

She stared up at him, not sure what he was talking about. "What?"

"I told you," he said. "I know all about babies. I'll go with you to the hospital."

He was offering to go with her and help. This was a novel experience for her and she liked it, but all the same, she didn't trust it. "Why would you want to do that?" she asked him warily.

His smile was more genuine than any she'd seen him give before. "I like babies. I . . ." He shrugged, looking slightly embarrassed. "I like you."

She stared a second longer. "Get out of here," she said, still suspicious.

He laughed and took her arm. "That's exactly what we're both going to do," he told her. "Let's get to the hospital and see that baby."

She let him lead her out to the car, but she wouldn't let him take his truck. "We'll go in my car," she said firmly. "This baby is coming home in style."

He settled into the passenger seat, only half listening to her nervous chatter as they drove toward the hospital. In his head and heart he was trying to assimilate what was happening. The moment of truth was here and he wasn't ready for it.

They parked and went into the visitors' lobby.

"Let's go see Jenny first," Sara told him, then hesitated. She knew she'd never mentioned that Jenny was her sister. "I *did* tell you she's my sister, didn't I?" she said brightly.

He took a deep breath. "Is she?" he said, his gaze hooded.

She nodded. "Yes. I'm adopting my sister's baby. Do you want to come and meet her?"

He shook his head slowly. "No, not really. You go on up and see her. I'll go down to the nursery and see how the baby is doing. I'll tell them you're ready to take her home."

"All right." Sara gave his hand a quick squeeze and smiled at him. "Thanks. You're really being great about this," she said, not noticing the frown her words brought to his eyes. "I'll meet you down in the nursery," she agreed, and took off for the elevator.

She had no idea what she was going to say to her sister. In all these months of planning and anticipating, she'd hardly believed this was really going to happen. And now it was here. She was going to have a baby, a sweet little child to raise all by herself. She was petrified.

She found the room and went right in, afraid that if she stopped she wouldn't be able to do it. There was Jenny looking tired but pretty, sitting on the side of the hospital bed in a pink robe and huge fuzzy slippers.

She flipped back her long, auburn hair when she saw Sara coming and smiled. "Hi, Mom," she said. "Have you seen your baby yet?"

Sara had been rushing toward her, but something in Jenny's words stopped her dead in her tracks and a painful lump rose in her throat.

"Jenny. Oh Jenny, I—"

Her sister put out a hand to stop her. "No obsequious gratitude, if you please. I hate slobbering."

"But when I think of what you've done..."

Jenny shook her head, searching her sister's eyes. "You may have been the one who talked me into doing this, Sara, but I knew all along it was the right thing to do. I couldn't have gone through with the abortion."

Sara nodded. She'd known that, too.

"And when you said you would take my baby, that made it so much easier." Jenny laughed suddenly, her eyes sparkling. "Not that it was all that easy. You've ruled my life for the last six months. You've told me what to eat, when to sleep, how to act. You made me play classical music to my belly, for Pete's sake."

Sara nodded. It was all true. She'd read the books and told Jenny what to do, and Jenny had groused and complained every step of the way. But Jenny was looking relieved now, and she rose and pulled down a suitcase and began throwing things into it.

"And now it's over, Sara," she said as she tucked away a magazine and some spare soap. "I'm free. You've got your baby. I'm out of here."

It finally got through to Sara that her sister was packing as though she were on the verge of walking out of the hospital and out of her life. "What are you doing? You just had a baby."

"I know. Believe me, I know."

"But where are you going?"

"Florida. Jake races power boats. We've got a big race coming up and we've got a lot to do before we leave."

Off to Florida. Jenny was always off to do something or go someplace exotic. It was astounding to think they had come from the same family. Where Sara was careful and craved perfection, Jenny was careless and craved excitement. Though they had never been close, Sara realized, suddenly, that she was going to miss her.

"I was hoping you would come to the baby shower," she said tentatively.

Jenny turned and looked at her, mouth twisted cynically. "No, you weren't. You don't want me there."

"Jenny, of course I do."

"No, you don't. My darling sister, your capacity for playing Let's Pretend is awesome. If I came to the shower, you would have to tell all your snooty friends your sister had an illegitimate baby, which you are now adopting. And you don't want to do that, do you?''

She was absolutely right, still . . . ''Jenny, please.''

''Sara, I know you better than you think. We were never real pals, you and I. You never really wanted to be a part of our family.''

''Well, look at what our family was like.''

''Our parents were a mess. So what? Nobody's perfect.'' She patted her sister's cheek with quick affection. ''Not even you.''

''I know that.''

Jenny laughed softly. ''You know it with your head, but in your heart, you still think perfection is possible if you just try hard enough.''

Sara drew herself up. ''Jenny, I think you're exaggerating. I'm not demented.''

''I never said you were. Despite everything, I actually love you. And I think you love me.''

Sara shook her head as though astounded her sister would even bring it up. ''Of course I do.''

Jenny started to laugh, but it turned into something else too quickly. ''I mean for real, Sara,'' she said, her voice slightly broken. ''Not just so it will look good.''

Suddenly there were tears in Sara's eyes and she nodded speechlessly. The two women came together in a hug that seemed to go on and on, both of them sobbing and clinging together.

When they finally drew back, both groping for tissues to clean up from the storm, they looked at each other and laughed softly. Then Jenny made her final speech to her sister.

''This baby is yours now,'' she said, her words heartfelt. ''All yours. I won't be back for a while, and

when I do come, I won't look at her as part of me.
She'll be your child. That's just the way it will always
be. Because, Sara, if it weren't for you, she wouldn't
exist today. You know that. I was contemplating an
abortion. You're the one who made me look at what
that really meant. You saved Calli's life. She belongs
to you."

Her words echoed in Sara's head and the tears
spilled over, blinding her. She had her little baby. Now
she had to go and see what she looked like.

The hospital corridor seemed to go on forever, and
then Drey heard the babies. He rounded a corner and
there they were. There was glass between the hallway
and the nursery, but you could hear the vocal ones. He
looked in and grinned. Babies affected him that way.
They always made him smile.

He started reading the cards stuck in the top of each
bassinet, looking for one that said "Kirkland." There
were twelve or thirteen of the little wigglers on view at
the moment. They came in all colors and all person-
alities. One baby was throwing so much of himself
into the screaming, his face was purple. A couple were
sleeping peacefully, their tiny faces calm and serene
despite the racket the others were making. One little
guy seemed to be talking to himself, fussing a bit,
blowing bubbles.

And then his gaze hit the baby he was looking for.
"Kirkland Baby" the card said. Without realizing it,
he held his breath as he slowly looked lower, into the
little bed. There lay the most beautiful baby he'd ever
seen. Light wisps of golden hair covered her head. Her
eyes were open wide and seemed to be staring right at
him. Her cheeks were round and pink and her little

chubby arms were waving, tiny fingers clutched into tight fists. The perfect lips formed a circle, and as her eyes met his, her arms began to rotate faster, as though she were revving up to fly into his arms.

He felt as though his heart had stopped. "I'm dreaming," he muttered. He'd seen newborn babies before. They never looked like this. He was imagining things—wasn't he? He was projecting—wasn't he? Had to be.

"Is she yours?" a friendly nurse asked, stopping to watch as he stared at the baby. "She's gorgeous. Talk about your perfect baby. She came out as though she were already six months old, didn't she?"

Turning, he stared at the woman as though she'd just dropped down out of a flying saucer to stand next to him. He didn't say a word. He was still too stunned to speak. His heart was beating so hard he was sure everyone in the place could hear it.

"New daddy, huh?" the nurse said, laughing and patting his arm. "Don't worry. You'll get used to it."

She walked around him and into the nurses' bay. He followed her.

"Excuse me," he said. His thought processes were crystal clear now, but he still wasn't sure what he should do. "About the birth certificate . . ."

"Oh, you won't get that for a couple of weeks. We put the information into the computer." She gestured toward a worn-looking model sitting on the desk. "It goes to the county. They send you your official copy."

"I see." He had no idea if Jenny had identified him as the father or not. If she hadn't, he wouldn't be able to do anything without hiring a lawyer. If she had, well, that was another story. If she had, he had as much right to decide what would happen to their baby as she did. Didn't he?

"Of course, we send the new mothers home with little hospital certificates, with the baby's foot prints on the back and all that."

"Oh. What information does that have on it?"

"The usual. Time and date of birth, weight, height, name. You know."

"Mother and father's names?"

She shook her head. "No, we don't put that on. Sometimes the mother doesn't want the father's name bandied about, you know, and this is a certificate she can show her friends and relatives. It's real cute."

"Great." He turned back to look at the babies, relieved. There was no way Sara would know he was the father until the birth certificate came. As long as Jenny didn't say anything to her. And he doubted Jenny would.

The nurse rose from the computer where she'd been entering data and answered the telephone, then left the room in a hurry. Drey took the opportunity to step quickly to the computer and take a look. He hit a key on the keyboard and the entire form came onto the screen. There was Calli's weight and length and Jenny's name. And there, in the slot for the father's identity, it said, father unknown.

Father unknown. He stared at it, hardly breathing.

He could easily fit in the correct response. No one was looking. It would only take seconds and he could put in his name and take complete control of this situation. He glanced back into the nursery, craned his head to see Calli's bed. The only thing visible from this angle were her little fists waving in the air. His heart lurched and he shook his head, looking back at the screen. No matter what the form said, he was Calli's father and no one would ever be able to take that away from him. All he had to do was make his claim. Blood tests would confirm it. He could take her with him if he wanted to. He could take her right now.

The nurse came back but she was taking another telephone call. He walked carefully to the entrance to the nursery and looked in. Calli was only steps away. He could reach her in seconds, take her up into his arms, and . . .

"Drey?"

Sara was there, her eyes wide with anticipation. "Drey? Which one is she?"

He stared at her for a moment. Should he tell her the truth? Should he do it now? The urge was there. This was his baby. Should he tell her Calli was his and he hadn't decided if he was going to let her go and be raised by a single mother? Should he throw her off the trail with some bogus information and take Calli up into his arms and get her out of here? All things were possible. What he had to do was figure out what would work best.

"Drey?" She put a hand on his arm, looking alarmed. "What is it? Is something wrong?"

His own hand covered hers and he stared down at her, his dark eyes intense. "This is it, Sara," he said. "Are you sure? Have you thought this through? Do you really want to take on this commitment?" He pulled her closer, searching her eyes, her face.

"It's a giant step. It's a walk off a cliff and there's no guarantee there's a net waiting below."

She smiled up at him, feeling shaky but serene. "Don't you get it, Drey?" she said. "I'm the net builder. I'm always building nets. I'm going to be okay. You just wait and see.''

He didn't know. He wasn't sure. He stared down at her and wished he could see into the future.

But she had no doubts. Turning, she looked eagerly toward the nursery. "Where is she?" she asked breathlessly.

The nurse got involved and soon came out with Calli in her arms. "Here you go. Here's your little one." She offered her for inspection, propping her up on her arm. "Isn't she pretty?"

Pretty wasn't the word for it. She was gorgeous, exquisite, ethereal, as beautiful as a heavenly angel and as lovable as a puppy. Sara thought her heart had stopped at the sight of her. This was going to be her baby. She felt as though she were moving in slow motion, as though her voice were long and low and strange.

"Can I hold her?" she was saying, and she could see her own hands reach out to take her, see them as though she were standing apart and watching someone else. It seemed to take forever to get her, to take her from the nurse. And then she was there. Sara had her.

The baby was impossibly small and incredibly sweet. Sara held her awkwardly, realizing this was probably the first baby she'd ever held.

"Careful not to let the head fall," the nurse advised her quickly. "Here, hold your hand behind the neck like this."

Sara shifted her hands, biting her lip with concentration, and the little face began to crumple.

"No, don't cry," she said anxiously, and the baby's opaque blue eyes shut as she did just that. The pudgy arms waved, and little feet began to kick. And the baby wailed at the top of her lungs.

"What do I do? What do I do?" Sara looked for help from Drey, but it was the nurse who took the baby back from her.

"There's nothing to it. Just hug her a little and pat her back a little." The nurse plopped the baby in place expertly against her shoulder and in no time at all, baby Calli had calmed and was sighing happily again.

"You see? That's the way. Now you try it."

It was no use. She'd stiffened up by now. The baby could feel it and the baby didn't like it at all. The minute Calli sensed she was back in Sara's arms, she began to take quick, sobbing breaths, getting ready to launch into the crying again.

"Don't worry, you'll get used to her and she'll get used to you," the nurse said, laughing as though it really weren't important. "Listen, put her back down while we finish up the paperwork. Then you can take her home."

Sara did as she'd suggested, laying the baby in her bassinet and backing away, but she felt utter dread inside, total failure. She wasn't doing this right. The baby knew she had no experience and the baby didn't like it.

Turning, she looked at Drey, her face a mask of tragedy, but she didn't say a word. Instead, she went along with the nurse to sign her name to documents.

Drey stood where he was, watching Sara leave the room, then turning back to watch Calli. "Hey, little girl," he whispered to her. "I've got to decide what to do with you."

The baby went very still and stared up at him. Suddenly a loud burp exploded from her rosebud mouth. He grinned.

"Watch it, kid," he murmured, reaching out to touch one little fist with his finger. "Show some respect to your old man."

Calli yawned and her eyes closed. In half a second, she was asleep.

"Uh-oh," Drey said, his humor fading. "This one is going to be a pistol. No doubt about it."

But that didn't help him to decide. As he heard Sara and the nurse coming back, he knew it was too late. For now, at any rate. There was always tomorrow.

Five

Sara drove home and Drey sat in the back next to the baby seat, which was strapped in so that Calli rode backward. It was the only way they could do it. Whenever Calli saw Sara, she howled. When she saw Drey, she brightened again, giving him a look as though she were glad he'd come to save her from the ugly meanie.

So far, Sara was keeping a stiff upper lip about the rejection, but Drey wondered how long she could keep it up. He knew how much it had to hurt. And so far, she hadn't made a sign that it bothered her. Hopefully, things would get better when they got Calli home.

Home. He glanced at the baby and winced. Was Sara's home going to be Calli's? The problem was, he didn't seem to be able to make up his mind. Didn't he know Sara well enough yet? How close did he have to get? How much was he willing to risk?

He stirred restlessly in the seat and tried to settle his mind, but thoughts kept tumbling into it. Before he made up his mind, maybe he should look into other alternatives. Maybe he should call children's services and see what kind of couples were waiting for babies right now. After all, he had to make sure he did the best thing possible for this baby. If he didn't do it, who would? Certainly not Jenny. Knowing her, she was probably relieved just to have this ordeal over with. It was up to him as Calli's only protector. He had to decide.

Maybe he was too close to the situation. Maybe he needed some distance. Whatever. Once they got Calli home and settled in, he would go. If he could get away from Sara and stand back, maybe he could see things more clearly. The whole thing was crazy anyway. He'd known this woman for less than twenty-four hours and already he was inextricably entangled in her life.

He glanced out the car window and noticed the scenery seemed to be passing in slow motion. "You know, the speed limit is forty-five through here," he reminded her.

She nodded, her eyes glued to the road. "I know, but I want to be careful. I want to get this baby home in one piece."

A huge truck passed them, leaving their car to shudder in its wake.

"You're going to be so careful we're going to get mowed down by traffic coming in from behind," Drey said. "Come on. This little girl is born to be wild. Aren't you, Calli?" He touched the downy head, feeling a stab of affection for the infant. "She wants to feel the wind in her hair."

Sara chuckled. "She doesn't have any hair. Or not enough to taunt the wind with, anyway."

Sara looked at the two of them in her rearview mirror and smiled. Drey was so good with her. She was going to have to watch him and learn how to do it. He looked up and caught her gaze, and she looked back at the road. But something tantalizing had sparked between them in the mirror and she couldn't deny it.

He Tarzan, me Jane, she thought to herself sensibly. And that is all there is to it.

But some little part of her denied it was that simple—and that temporary. Some hormonal pot was simmering and pretty soon it was going to be ready to blow. She didn't know how she knew that, because it wasn't in her experience at all. But she knew it all the same. And she didn't know how long she was going to be able to let Drey hang around. She might have to ask him to go, just for her own peace of mind.

She pulled into her driveway, a thread of excitement beating in her throat. Here she was, home with her baby. Turning in the seat, she smiled at Drey and wondered why she felt so comfortable with him involved. She hardly knew him. And yet, in some ways she felt she'd known him all her life.

They carried the baby up into the perfect little baby bedroom and put her in the perfect little bassinet, all decorated with yellow ribbons and white lace.

The best that money can buy, Drey thought to himself. But was that enough?

They stood side by side and looked down at her. She was halfway between sleep and wakefulness, her little eyes drooping as her attention traveled from one face to the other. Slowly Sara turned her gaze to meet Drey's dark eyes.

"Now what?" she asked anxiously. "What do I do?"

Drey gave her a fleeting smile. "Now you wait."

"Wait?" She glanced down at Calli again. Her little eyes had closed. She was sleeping, and Sara took the hint, backing away from the bassinet and going on in a whisper. "Wait for what?"

He took her arm and began to lead her quietly from the room. "You wait for the baby to wake up," he advised with a twinkle in his dark eyes.

Sara frowned as they made their way toward the stairs. "And then what do I do?"

He stopped at the top of the stairs and smiled down at her. "You wait for her to go back to sleep again."

Sara glared at him suspiciously, not as gullible as he might think. There seemed to be a pattern developing here. "That's all there is to it? You wait for her to wake up and then you wait for her to sleep again?"

Drey hesitated, as though he had more information but wasn't sure if she was ready to face it just yet. "Well, there are other things you do," he admitted at last. "They're sort of interspersed between the two types of waiting."

She knew very well she was being teased, but she bit none the less. "And just what are they?"

He shrugged, holding back a smile. "You feed her. And you change her diapers."

Sara nodded, tapping her foot. "So it's food in, waste out. Sleep in, sleep out." Folding her arms across her chest, she faced him with her head to the side. "And that, in your experienced opinion, is the sum of my days from now on?"

He smiled, but his eyes were watchful. This was more than pure teasing. He was also testing her, and he wondered if she didn't guess it at times. "Just about. You now know the secret of motherhood. The question is, are you prepared to meet this challenge?"

She shook her head, giving him an exasperated look. "You are a cynical man." Putting her nose in the air, she defied him as she began to descend the stairs. "I refuse to be confined by those boundaries."

He shrugged one shoulder as he followed her. "So now you're a rebel? And just what are you going to do to go against the conventions?"

She hesitated at the door to the kitchen, thinking of the sweet little face. "I'm going to read to her. I'm going to take her to the park and let her feel the sun on her face. I'm going to sing to her and talk to her."

Drey watched her, saw the emotion as she spoke, and he was impressed. It was obvious she'd been thinking about this. She'd probably been reading books and talking to people. At least she wasn't going into it casually. That was a factor to throw into the equation.

Then she went one step too far, making him groan and shake his head.

"I want to be the perfect mother," she declared at the end of her speech, making it an anthemlike statement with her head held high and her blue eyes shining. "I want to do everything just right."

But Drey frowned. "Calli doesn't need the perfect mother," he said with gruff emphasis. "She needs a human mother. She needs love." Drey looked at Sara in exasperation. Why this constant need for appearances? "Perfection she can do without."

"No, you don't understand," Sara began.

But he didn't let her get started. "I think I understand only too well. You're trying to make the world around you perfect to make up for something in your past. I don't know if something happened in your childhood or something is lacking in your adult life, or what. But you obviously feel the need to make up for something. And it's time you faced it and dealt with it."

His words shocked her. She knew he was right—she'd always known these things—and yet, she didn't appreciate him trying to teach her about herself. She blinked at him for a moment, then turned coolly and went into the kitchen, reaching for the kettle to make some tea.

"What are you doing, trying out your wings as an amateur psychologist?" she asked icily.

He followed her in and slid onto a bar stool at the counter. "Come on," he said, leaning on it. "It's just common sense."

She whirled and glared at him. "Oh, now not only do I have a troubled past, I have no common sense."

He groaned as she went back to making the tea, her every movement just a little too sharp, with pots banging a little too loudly and cups hitting the tiled countertop with a crack. She was miffed and he couldn't blame her. If only he could think of a way to put his concerns into words that explained but didn't sting. He tried once more.

"Listen, what I'm trying to tell you is—you've done the perfection bit. You've probably been perfect for years. Ask anybody. I bet the world stands back and looks at you in awe half the time." He counted off her virtues on the fingers of his left hand. "You never forget an appointment, never have a leaf on your driveway, never have a bad hair day." These were not circumstances he'd seen for himself, but he'd heard things, and he could extrapolate from what he'd seen of her. "You've done perfection and you've done it magnificently. It's time to move on."

She leaned on the counter across from him and gave him a sharp look. "Move on to what?"

He leaned toward her, looking deep into her eyes. "To being real," he said softly. "To putting openness and love above perfection."

She stared back, wishing she knew how. "So now you're an amateur philosopher," she said evasively. "You're a real Renaissance man, aren't you?"

He hesitated. It was tempting to go on, to give her a long, deep lecture, but he knew there was a time when you hit a point of diminishing returns, and the object of your moral lesson tuned you out. She'd given him an opening to go for a lighter approach, and he followed it.

"That's me," he said. "At home in the woods or at the ballet. You name it, I can do it." He shrugged, looking pleased with himself. "Or at least I know where to hire someone to get it done."

She smiled her relief, glad he seemed willing to leave the subject of her supposed neurosis behind. "Hire me a genie, would you? I'd like to make a few wishes."

He shook his head slowly. "No can do. The genie union is on strike this week. They're demanding lava lamps in place of the old oil versions. If you really need something done, you've got me."

Her smile softened. "Do you grant wishes?" she asked him.

"All the time. What is your heart's desire?"

Her smile turned tremulous. "That Calli be happy. That she love me and grow up straight and tall. That I do this right."

He wanted to comfort her, but he wasn't sure how to do it. "I can't tell if that's one wish or three," he said softly.

She turned away, afraid she was going to start blubbering if she wasn't careful. She never cried in front of people. Never. She'd done all her crying in that little closet in her childhood. There was the tea to deal with, and she used it to hide from him for a moment.

"Anyway," he said for lack of anything better to say, "if wishes were fishes, blind pigs would fly, or something like that."

"What?" She turned back and gave out a sputtering laugh. "You've got it all wrong."

"Cut me some slack," he said carelessly. "I'm just learning this genie stuff. I'll do better next time."

She smiled, shaking her head, and he rose from the stool and reached into his toolbox, which was sitting on the floor in the corner. Pulling out his tool belt, he strapped it on.

"I think I'll go up and finish the plans that were interrupted last night," he told her.

"Don't make any noise," she said anxiously.

"Don't worry," he said, turning to go. "They can sleep through a hurricane at this age."

"But I have to be able to hear her if she cries. And if you make noise, I won't be able to tell if it's her."

"Ah. Of course." He started for the stairs.

She stood watching him, smiling at the way he looked, so macho and male and ready for anything. He turned and caught her at it.

"What?" he said, pausing at the foot of the stairs.

"You," she said, feeling a sudden rush of affection for him. "You look like one of those guys on the calendars," she said, chuckling.

His look was one of complete horror. "What?"

"Oh, not the cheesy dancers. The ones where they have real guys. Postmen of Peoria, or Handsome Hunks Who Handle Hardware. You've seen them."

He shook his head. "Not in my worst nightmares."

"They're darling. How about we do one of you called the County's Cutest Carpenters?"

"Give me a break," he said, but a slight flush appeared on his cheeks and she realized, to her amazement, that she was embarrassing him. Here he was, Mr. Know-it-all, about to start blushing. She smiled wickedly. She had no pity at all.

"It might be fun," she teased. "We could pose you without your shirt on. Maybe just dressed in your tool belt."

He turned and began to take the stairs two at a time. "I'm out of here," he muttered as he fled.

"How about Cuddly Carpenters and Wild Woodworkers?" she called after him, giggling. She went to the bottom of the stairs and called up, "Which one would you rather be?"

He looked back down. "How about Cantankerous Carpenters Who Can't Take Kidding?" he said grumpily. "In the meantime, color me gone." And he disappeared into the bedroom.

Her smile faded as he left her line of sight. How was it that a man like Drey could be so responsive, so easy to talk to, easy to like, and so filled with empathy for what she was going through, when a man like Craig, with all the wealth and background and education in the world, could be so cold?

She poured herself another cup of tea and sat down. She needed time to think, time to settle her nerves and her heart rate. Everything in her had been going a mile a minute since she'd had the phone call that morning telling her Calli had been born. It was really true. She had a baby sleeping in a room upstairs, and she was all hers. She didn't know whether she was more excited or scared. Both, probably, in equal measure.

It was so lucky Drey had been there to help her. There was something about him, something rock solid and, at the same time, mercilessly dangerous that kept her on edge no matter how much she depended upon him.

"Everything is scaring you, you scaredy-cat," she muttered to herself.

It was time to call in the nurse. She needed her for security, and she knew darn well Drey wouldn't stay forever. After all, he was just the carpenter. Wasn't he? Sometimes it was hard to remember that.

The pool man finally showed up and was outside cleaning the pool. There were two calls from Dr. Bracken on the answering machine, and she called his nurse to give him the message that she was fine today. She put a call in to Ginger Cates who ran her import-export firm when Sara was off doing other things. Ginger assured her all was going well and she wasn't to think about business until things had settled down with the new baby. She blessed the woman and gave herself a pat on the back for having hired her six months before. Busying herself with a few bills and other phone calls, she tried to put the shower back in focus in her mind.

It was almost an hour later when a sound came from the baby's room and she whirled. Any sound from now on, she knew, was going to send her flying. She raced up the stairs and tiptoed into the room. Even from the doorway she could see one little fist waving in the air.

Her heart filled with love and she went quickly to the bassinet, looking down.

"Hello, darling," she said. "You beautiful baby."

The little blue eyes stared at her hard. At first they didn't seem to focus, and Sara cooed to her again. But then Calli seemed to realize who this was, and slowly the little face began to crumple.

"No, oh no. Don't cry. Oh, please don't cry!"

Sara very carefully took the little bundle up into her arms and held her a little less awkwardly than she had done at the hospital.

"Hush now, don't you cry," she whispered, rocking her gently. But heart-wrenching sobs began racking the little body, and then full-fledged crying began to rock the room.

Frustration was building in Sara's heart but she tried to remain calm, patting the baby softly, murmuring sweet nothings in its little shell-like ear. But nothing seemed to work, and a feeling of dread began to seep in.

It seemed to take forever for Drey to arrive on the scene. She knew he was probably hanging back to let her try to calm the baby herself. But it wasn't working. Nothing was working. She watched with relief as he came into the room, knowing his touch would do the trick.

He took the baby from her and the crying began to lose its volume immediately. He held her close and cooed something into her ear, little soft baby non-sense words, and she quieted. In another moment, Calli was relaxed, obviously delighted to be with him, near him, the center of his attention. Sara watched enviously. She had to learn how to do that.

"What she wants is to be changed and fed," he told her, leading the way to the changing table. "There's no mystery here."

He was trying to make her feel better about the way Calli was reacting, and Sara appreciated it, but it didn't change anything. She helped put on fresh diapers and warmed the bottle while Drey held the little one. He started the feeding, and while Calli was engrossed, slowly transferred her to Sara's arms. Sara took her carefully. She'd never felt anything so wonderful as this small package of life. Everything went fine until she couldn't resist whispering something endearing. Calli's eyes shot open and she drew back from the bottle as though she were sure she was being poisoned.

"It's okay," Sara said calmly. "You just go on drinking."

To her surprise, Calli did. But she watched Sara out of the corners of her eyes the entire time, and when the bottle was empty, she wanted Drey again.

Sara followed and watched while he burped her and put her back down in her little bed.

"You're a spellbinder, aren't you?" she said softly to him, half jealous, half admiring. "Dream weaver. You have a magic touch."

His mouth quirked. "All the women fall for me," he noted, glancing at her teasingly. "It's my special talent. I'm surprised you hadn't noticed before."

She tried to smile, pulling her arms in tightly. "I did notice you had a certain appeal. But I've been resisting it. And so far, I've done a pretty good job of it, don't you think?" She looked up.

His gaze caught in hers and he saw something there, something raw and naked, and his pulse began to beat just a little faster. His instinct was to move toward her, to reach out, to touch her, and he had to pull himself back and turn away, cursing under his breath.

This was exactly what he had to avoid. Imagine the complications that could arise if he actually got tangled up in some kind of relationship with Sara. He already had that affair with Jenny to atone for, and then the fact that he hadn't told Sara he was the father of the baby she was adopting. It was already too complicated. If he did anything to complicate it even further, the repercussions would go on forever. He had to stay away from her. One little slip, and he could find himself engulfed in a fire that would destroy everything.

"Maybe I should go," he said, turning back with a frown.

She shook her head, still facing him. She could sense something of what he was thinking, but she couldn't figure out why he was retreating. "You can't go," she said simply. "Not yet."

He risked looking into her crystal eyes. "Sara..."

She put a hand on his arm and looked up at him, her eyes melting with worry. "Please, Drey. You can't leave me alone with her. She...she doesn't love me yet."

He glanced back at where Calli was drowsily drifting into sleep. What if she never did? What if it just didn't work out between the two of them? Would he take her then?

"She'll get used to you soon," he told her, sorry that that was the best he could do. "I should leave the two of you alone to work this out." He left the room and went along the hallway, heading for the stairs.

Sara shook her head as she followed him. Before he started down, she caught his arm again, holding him back. "You can't go until she's ready to accept me. It's not fair to her. She'll be scared."

He looked deeply into her eyes, searching them, wondering. There was no self-pity there, just pure determination. She had her goal in front of her and she wasn't going to waver from it. He had to admire that, admire her. She deserved a baby to love her. Was she going to get this one? It was pretty much up to him and he wasn't at all sure. Maybe the way Calli was acting was a sign. Maybe this situation wasn't right for her.

"Teach me," she said, still staring up into his eyes.

He moved uncomfortably. "Teach you what?"

"How to hold her so that she'll love me."

"Sara..." His heart broke for her.

"Drey, don't you see? I have to get her to love me."

"She will." He had no way of knowing, no business promising her that. Still he couldn't help it. She needed so much.

But she was stronger than he was. She didn't accept his words.

"You can't know that," she said calmly. "It doesn't happen just because you want it to." She hesitated, then lifted her chin bravely and went on, telling this man she hardly knew things she hadn't told anyone before. "I . . . I tried for five years to get Craig to love me and he never did."

He stared at her, stunned, not sure he could believe what he'd heard her say. "Craig?" he repeated. "Your husband?"

She nodded, pressing her lips together. "We had a sort of marriage of convenience. I didn't know that at first, but I found out soon enough. I always hoped it would turn into more, but it never did. He just couldn't bring himself to love me."

Anger shot through him, a rage so great, if he could have gotten his hands on the man, he would have been hard-pressed to keep from beating him to a pulp. "Craig must have been crazy," he told her fiercely, his voice rough. "Believe me, you are infinitely lovable."

Her wide eyes stared up into his. "How can I believe that when no one has ever really loved me?" she whispered to him.

"Believe it, Sara," he said, his voice rasping with deep emotion. "You would be so damn easy to love."

He knew he shouldn't say it, shouldn't do it. He knew he should stay away. But he had to show her. He had to wipe that pain from her eyes.

He pulled her to him almost angrily, his hands holding her face up toward his. He took her mouth as though he meant to prove something, coming down hard and firm, making a statement. But it took only moments for his toughness to melt into desire. She was softer than he'd expected, warmer, sweeter, and once he'd found that out, he realized one kiss wasn't going to be enough. Maybe twenty weren't.

He pulled her closer, wanting to feel her breasts against his chest, wanting to hold her slim frame closer to him. She bent to his control in a way he wouldn't have thought possible, opening to him, inviting more, almost leading him on, and his blood began to move more quickly through his veins, pumping excitement, beating time to a dance that beckoned from the shadows, tempting him to go further, to reach higher, to press harder.

Her arms slid around his neck, letting her arch into him, making the seal between their bodies complete. His thoughts began to blur and his instincts began to take over, making him forget his promises to himself, his reasons for being here. He wanted her with a dull, aching urgency that filled his body and wiped out his intelligence. As his hands slipped beneath her shirt and made their way down under her waistband, filling his senses with the feel of her naked flesh, he forgot everything but raw, basic hunger for her.

It was up to her to stop things, and she did. But it wasn't easy. It had been years and years since any man had shown with his body that he might find her seductive and it was hard not to glory in it. At the same time, it was a little scary. She wasn't very practiced at this sort of thing and she wasn't sure she knew how she was supposed to react.

Naturally, something inside her said. She should just do what felt right.

But she didn't trust that voice. She seldom did what came naturally. She did what would look good. And she knew this wasn't it.

"Hey," she said breathlessly, pulling back from his strong embrace. "I get the picture. Thanks for the vote of confidence."

He stared down at her for a moment as though he hardly knew who she was or what she was saying. His breath was slightly rough in his throat and it took him a minute to regain his equilibrium. When he did, he drew back, blinking as though at a bright sun.

What the hell was going on here? It wasn't like him to do a thing like this. What was it about this woman that made him forget his scruples, forget his maturity, forget even his humanity, for God's sake?

He stepped back, afraid to stay too close, and she laughed softly, touching his arm to reassure him.

"I didn't tell you that—about Craig—because I wanted you to do what you just did," she told him earnestly.

"I know that," he said, but his eyes didn't say that at all. He looked wary of her, as though he just weren't sure.

She bit her lip, worried about the way he was reacting. "I don't want you to think..."

He took her shoulders in his hands and shook his head, looking into her eyes. "Sara, I'm not thinking right now. I'm running on pure adrenaline. Don't expect rational thought. It's not available at the moment."

She nodded quickly, but she was startled to think their kisses had really affected him strongly. It was a little thrilling and very bizarre. He was such a beautiful, sexy man. Did he really want her? And if so, why hadn't Craig?

Six

Drey went back to work on his shelves and Sara went down to the kitchen to fix something for dinner. She was walking on air and she knew why.

"You're dreaming if you think anything is going to come of this," she told herself scornfully. But weren't dreams what life was made of?

Calli woke up and stayed awake for the rest of the afternoon. Drey played with her and tried to get her to play with Sara. She got better about it. At least, when Sara smiled and cooed at her, she didn't yell back. But when it came to holding, she wanted Drey's arms around her.

"Well, who wouldn't?" Sara muttered to herself. Still it stung.

She got out all the cute little stretch suits she'd bought to put the baby in, just to make herself feel a little better. She put the cutest one, striped like a tiger cub, on her child and took pictures while Drey propped her up. They watched every move she made, every expression, every sound, and laughed and looked at each other with delight over everything she did.

"She's perfect," Sara said again and again. "I can hardly wait to show her off at the shower."

They were in the baby's room and she was going through all the baby clothes she'd been collecting, putting things in piles, organizing Calli's very new life for her.

Drey had the baby up against his shoulder, where she was gurgling and trying to burp. Sara glanced at her and smiled. She was going to get to that point with Calli, where the baby would accept her new mother with quiet pleasure. She was bound and determined to make it happen and she had no doubt it would, even though she was getting a bit impatient.

"What's the deal with this shower thing?" Drey asked at last. She'd mentioned it so many times he was beginning to realize just how important it must be to her.

"I'm having a shower to welcome the baby," she told him happily. "My closest friends are coming in from all over the country for it."

He frowned. Something seemed just a little odd about this. "Don't other people usually give the new mother the shower? You're having this one for yourself?"

"Yes," she replied with sunny unconcern. "I put a note saying 'no gifts, please' on the invitation, if that's what you're worried about."

"But some will still bring gifts."

"Sure they will. Some people love to bring gifts to babies, regardless of whether it's a shower or not." She grinned at him. "Do you really think I'm having this whole thing as a way to get gifts? There are easier ways to do that, believe me."

He shook his head. "That's not it. It just seems strange." He'd been about to suggest she have Jenny do it for her, but then held his tongue.

"There's no one else to have it for me," she said matter-of-factly.

"But if you have all these friends..."

She shook her head, folding more little suits into stacks. "No one in Denver. No one that close." Turning up her face, she looked at him thoughtfully. It was odd, but this new openness she was trying to achieve with the world seemed perfectly natural with Drey. Sometimes she felt she could tell him almost anything.

"I...well, I've been through a lot lately and I feel that I need my real friends, my oldest friends, to come together and help me celebrate this new life I'm embarking on."

"This new life with this innocent little baby," he murmured, thinking things through as he bounced Calli against his shoulder and patted her gently.

"Yes." She frowned, looking at him. "Why do you say it that way?"

But he wasn't listening. Coming to her side of the room, he leaned against the dresser, shifting Calli from one shoulder to the other. "Let me get this straight. Your ex-husband is coming to your shower."

"Yes." She didn't see why that bothered him. It didn't seem odd to her at all. "Only no one knows he's an ex."

He frowned even more darkly. Her constant need to project ideal appearances was a total mystery to him. "You mean you're planning to present this picture of the perfect couple adopting the perfect baby to all your old friends?"

Her gaze was clear and bright as she looked into his eyes. "What's wrong with that?"

He threw up his free hand. "It's a lie, that's what's wrong."

She gasped, shocked. He really didn't get it and she resented his characterization of her plans. She'd never claimed she had perfection, she only claimed it as a goal, an aspiration, something out there in the realm of the ideal to shoot for. "No, it's not. It's the way things should be."

"Should be, maybe. But they're not."

He didn't understand. She stared at him for a long moment, realizing he probably never would. And how could she explain to him when she didn't really completely understand it all herself? She only knew that deep inside she had a driving need to show a facade of perfection to the world, especially to those she loved the best. Somehow it had to be acknowledged that she'd done things right, that it had turned out okay. At least, as okay as it could get.

"In other words," he said dryly, "what you're planning for your shower is a giant hoax."

She stopped folding and turned to face him. She should have known it was a mistake to tell him the truth, that all this talk about openness and honesty was just a trap. And now she knew she was going to live to regret it.

"This is something I have to do, Drey," she said quietly. "I'm sorry you don't approve, but it really doesn't matter. It's my shower. I'll do it my way."

He looked at her and he had to admit she was an impressive sight. Her jaw was set and her eyes were steady. There was a sense of determination in her he hadn't seen since his father had stopped the wind from blowing down the old apple tree in the yard by going out and holding on to it himself. All of a sudden he wanted to laugh. Yes, this was the real Sara Parker. If the world didn't give her the perfection she wanted, she would damn well force it to surrender eventually, come hell or high water.

"Okay, Sara," he said, his eyes shining with amusement. "Have your shower. Show the world how perfect your life is." He shook his head warningly. "But don't be surprised if the world isn't very interested in that. I'd be willing to bet that the people who love you only care whether or not you're happy, not how perfect you are or aren't."

Sara got the point and she appreciated that he gave it so good-naturedly. "I'll cross that bridge when I crash into it," she told him.

"I'll bet you will," he murmured, holding the little girl in his arms a little more tightly. She was asleep and he walked over and laid her down on her back. Her rosebud mouth fell open, but her eyes stayed closed. He looked down at her and tried very hard not to love her. *Don't do it,* his conscience warned. *You won't be able to turn away if you do.*

He hardened his heart. He wasn't going to let himself fall for this little angel any more than he could let himself fall for her new mother. It would be crazy to do it, and he wasn't that far gone.

"Hear that wind?" she said, turning her head as a tree brushed against the house. "It sounds so cold."

He nodded, feeling suddenly chilled. There was a storm coming. It was time to batten down the hatches.

They went down to have the light meal Sara had cooked for them. She had canned salmon with a light cream sauce and asparagus with rolls. He pronounced it delicious and she glowed with the praise, then marveled at the man. He could make her feel so good with just the touch of his hand, the look in his eye, and yet he went even further and said things that made her truly happy. When she'd lived with Craig, it seemed everything she did was wrong, everything she planned or cooked or set up had to be criticized and torn down again. If only she'd married a man like Drey, her life would have been very different.

And what kind of woman did Drey want? She speculated, watching him from across the table, and finally she asked. "Tell me about your girlfriend," she coaxed, her eyes deceptively bland and casual.

He raised one dark eyebrow and gave her a look. He knew prying when he ran into it. But he didn't mind. After all, he'd pried enough into her life, hadn't he? "What makes you think I have a girlfriend?" he said, knowing he was just delaying the issue.

She sighed and leaned on her elbows. "Well, I know you don't have a wife," she said.

He leashed his grin. "How do you know that?"

She smiled at him, her eyes twinkling. "No wife would let you keep your hair long like that."

His hand went to his golden locks, running through them. Funny, but that was exactly what he'd always known a wife would want to do—cut his hair. It seemed to be some sort of Samson and Delilah complex with them.

"You don't like my hair?" he asked as though he couldn't imagine such a thing occurring.

She waved a fork in the air. "I love your hair. It makes you look sexy, like Hercules or some wild West guy." She shook the fork at him. "But it's not like a husband."

"You've got that one right." He nodded slowly, his eyes warm as he watched her. "I'm not a husband. And I don't have a girlfriend, either."

She let the frown come back, mostly to hide the little burst of joy that had happened inside her at his words. It wouldn't do to let him know that was good news, would it? "Now that I find very hard to believe," she said.

He shrugged, sipping his wine and gazing at her from across the table. "I've been too busy working lately," he said with a provocative grimace. "I don't have time for women."

She nodded. "Me, too. I understand completely."

Since Craig, she hadn't even thought about it. Men seemed to be more trouble than they were worth. And all in all, she thought she'd made a good decision. She had a baby but no man to tell her she was doing it all wrong and that she had been stupid to try it in the first place. That was fine with her. But deep inside, a tiny squiggle of doubt still lingered. Was it really fair to Calli? Didn't she deserve a father just as much as any other little girl?

Drey raised an eyebrow. "So tell me, what's your ideal man like?" he asked.

"My ideal man is..." She tried to see him in her mind but for some strange reason, Drey's face kept getting in the way. "Tall, dark and handsome, I suppose," she told him, but it was a throwaway description and he knew it as well as she did.

"Would you marry again?" he asked, and this time he tensed, very interested in the answer.

She hesitated, though she didn't notice his interest. Then she shrugged, surprising herself with her answer. "Sure. If I could find the right man."

The right man. Yes, that was the key, wasn't it? The right man would improve things instead of tearing them down. Why hadn't she thought of it that way before?

He nodded, watching her from under thick, dark eyelashes. "What kind of man would be right?" he asked softly.

She shrugged. It seemed self-evident to her. "Someone who was my type," she said sensibly.

His mouth twitched at the corners. "And what do you consider your type?"

She held his gaze and didn't waver. "Someone who is the opposite of you."

"Me?" He gazed at her, aghast. "What's so bad about me?"

She grinned and went for the joke instead of the truth. "Nothing a little haircut wouldn't fix."

He laughed and rose from the table, taking his dish to the sink. "Women. You're all alike, obsessed with appearances." Turning back to look at her, he added, "Thank you for a great meal. I guess I'll go back to work for another hour or so."

She didn't say a word as he left the room. They hadn't talked about what was going to happen tonight, about whether he would sleep in her house again. She knew she wanted him to. But how could she completely take over this man's life? It didn't seem very fair to him. And still...

He'd barely left the room when the telephone rang. She answered and found a tiny, very feminine voice on the other end of the line.

"Hi," said the voice. "This is Gigi. Is Drey there?"

Sara's heart gave a little lurch. No girlfriend, huh? Then what the heck was this? "Gigi?" she echoed stiffly.

"Yes. Do you want me to spell it?" The tone wasn't the least bit sarcastic. The woman really meant it. Still her offer rankled a bit.

"Spell it?" said Sara coolly. "I thought you already had."

"What?"

She didn't get it. Sara raised an eyebrow of her own. "Never mind. Drey is here. Did you want to talk to him?"

"Please."

"Just a moment."

She put down the receiver and walked to the stairs, moving slowly, deliberately. There was no way she was going to run.

She found Drey in the nursery, searching for studs in the wall. He was down to his light white T-shirt and all those delicious muscles were outlined seductively. She thought of volleyball and of sand turning to burning coals and bit her lip.

He looked up questioningly and she told him why she'd come. "Some little elf person is on the phone for you," she said airily.

"An elf person?" He gave her a wary look. "What are you talking about?"

She shrugged. "That's what she sounds like. And you were bragging about your prowess in the woods a little while ago."

Drey started to protest her characterization of things, then thought better of it and asked, instead, "What's her name?"

"Gigi." She said it with all the Maurice Chevalier accent she could muster.

"Gigi. Oh, damn." He glanced at his watch, looking truly chagrined. "I forgot."

"You can use the extension," she said, pointing to the telephone on the night table.

"Thanks," he said, moving quickly. Though she knew it was rude, Sara stayed right where she was standing. She wasn't going to give him his privacy. Not yet, she wasn't.

"I'm really sorry, Gigi," he said. "I got tied up here and I..." He paused, then grinned as though she'd said something funny.

"Oh. Okay." He laughed, sounding suddenly sultry. "No kidding. I think I can handle that. Sure. Give me half an hour. We'll go out for drinks. I know a little club downtown where there's a band and dancing. Yes, I know. You..."

He turned, obviously hoping to keep Sara from hearing the rest of his conversation. The move only made her strain harder to make sure she picked it up.

"You sound cute, too," he was saying. "I'll see you very shortly."

A blind date. That was obviously it. Well, what did she expect? Men like Drey didn't walk around loose for long. There was always someone trying to trap them into something. But did he have to be so sappy about it?

"Oh, please," she muttered, turning away.

"You shouldn't eavesdrop," he told her, his dark eyes shimmering with amusement. "You never hear things you want to."

She turned back and glared at him. "Didn't I tell you she was a forest creature?"

He grinned, enjoying her jealousy even though he knew very well it didn't mean a thing. "An elf, I think you said," he mused. "Yes, I can buy that. She had that kind of voice. Can't you just see her dancing in the sunbeams that glint in through the forest trees? Someone pretty and perky and—"

"Slimy and dirty and covered with moss," she added gruffly. "I suppose you're going to see her, aren't you? You can let me know which of us is closer to the truth."

His grin faded. "You don't mind, do you? I mean . . ."

She shook her head, looking at him in quiet wonder. "Of course I don't mind," she told him. "You've been wonderful helping me with Calli all day. I'm sure you do have a life out there in the world, people who you'd like to get back to." She smiled at him. "Anyway, the nurse is coming by in about an hour. She's not moving in until tomorrow, but she'll be here soon in case I'm going crazy."

"I'll be back by midnight," he assured her.

She looked at him in surprise and tried to hide the relief she felt. "Really? Are you sure?"

He stopped and looked down into her eyes. "Don't you want me to?" he asked her.

She hesitated. Everything in her wanted him back, wanted him to stay in the first place. But she couldn't let him see that. For appearance's sake, she should say something tart, act unconcerned, let him off the hook.

But, for once, she couldn't do that. Real emotion, honest feeling, came through instead. "Yes," she said softly, nodding her head and letting him see, for just a moment, everything she felt right in her eyes. "Yes, please come back."

He hesitated. Now he didn't really want to go. But he'd promised. And he would be back very soon. "I will," he told her solemnly. "You can count on me."

You can count on me.

The words echoed long after he'd left.

"I learned long ago not to count on anyone but myself," she told Calli as she gave her an evening bottle. The dark blue eyes stared up at her as though the little girl understood every word. "Now this big handsome man comes along and says, 'Count on me.' What do you think, Calli? Should I believe him?"

Not a chance, she told herself sensibly as she put Calli up against her shoulder and began pacing the room. He probably wouldn't be back until the next day. After all, he had a date with a forest elf. Who knew what that could lead to.

Calli made a delicate, ladylike burp and Sara laughed, holding her out where she could see her face. She was making progress. The baby didn't scream in her arms any longer, but she was still stiff and unyielding and, despite the immaturity of her reactions and expressions, Sara could see distrust in her little face. Sara's laughter faded and a twinge of pain shot through her instead.

She doesn't like me, she thought, tears threatening. She realized it had to be true and it broke her heart.

But she wasn't about to give up. "By hook or by crook, little girl," she whispered to her, shaking her head sadly. "You are going to learn to like me. It's in the cards. It's gotta be."

The eyes stared at her like stones, no emotion, no change.

The nurse came around seven. A tall, dour woman, she seemed capable and efficient.

"My name is Marta Marie Engles Tyler, but you may call me Mattie," she announced in a tone that said she was planning to take over.

"Fine, Mattie," Sara said in return. "And why don't you just call me Mrs. Parker?"

It was a formal touch she didn't usually ask for or want, but something about this woman told her she would have to work hard to keep the upper hand around her, and she decided she might as well start off with a move for dominance right away.

"I'm quite proud of the children I've helped raise. They've all turned out beautifully. And the reason it has all gone so well is this—I have a definite schedule. Every child must conform to it. I feed a baby once every four hours no matter what. Nothing in between feedings. Nap time is the same time every day. At six months, I insist there be no more waking up in the night. At nine months, the bottle gets thrown in the trash. We have a little ceremonial way of doing it so the child knows I'm serious. At fifteen months, the baby is potty trained or I'll know the reason why. At eighteen months, no more night diaper."

Sara stared at her. The battle for dominance was going to be harder than she'd thought. This schedule fetish sounded a little drastic, but what did she know? Nurse Mattie was supposed to be the expert.

"Now tell me this," the nurse said. "You are a single mother, right? I only deal with single mothers. No men, thank you very much. I can't abide them."

Sara nodded quickly. "Yes, it's just me and Calli. My ex-husband Craig will be dropping in next week for a few days, but for the rest, it's just us two."

The nurse looked at her sharply. "I won't stay with a man in the house," she warned.

"Just for a few days?" Sara asked anxiously. "I'm having a lot of people in for a shower on Saturday. All women, except for Craig," she added hurriedly. "Surely you can stand to be around one little man for a few days."

Mattie sniffed suspiciously. "We'll see about that," she warned. "I'll have to talk to him and see if he'll fit in with my plans."

Her plans—good grief! Sara hadn't realized hiring a nurse would be like hiring a dictator to take over her life.

And Mattie did take over right away, changing the way things were set up in the baby's room. Calli seemed to be as overwhelmed as Sara was. She didn't make a peep when the woman lifted her from her bed, and for the first time, she seemed to be looking toward Sara for reassurance that this buffalo of a woman wasn't going to hurt her.

"It's all right, baby," Sara cooed. "This is Nurse Mattie."

And Calli's little chin began to tremble.

She wants Drey, Sara thought, smiling sadly. What the heck—who didn't?

It drove her crazy to think about him out on a date. Especially with someone with such a wispy voice who went by the name of Gigi.

She's either French, she decided to herself, or she grew up on old movies and thinks of herself as a gamine. She sighed. And if she looked anything like Leslie Caron, they'd never see him again.

Which wouldn't be all that strange. After all, he was only the carpenter. Only the carpenter. Funny how that concept was becoming more and more outdated.

He wasn't only the carpenter at all. He was a strong, very attractive man who made her feel . . . what exactly did he make her feel? Alive? Awake? Desired? All things she hadn't felt much for a very long time. No wonder she liked him.

And that is all there is to that, she told herself firmly. Nothing more. If he never showed up again, she would hardly notice.

Nurse Mattie left, threatening to come back in the morning, and Sara wondered what she was going to do about that. Somehow she had a feeling this woman was not going to work out after all.

She put Calli down to sleep for the night and went down to the kitchen to brew herself some tea and think things over. She had a thousand things to think about, but the issue that kept dominating all others in her life was Drey. She frowned and shoved him away. She needed to think about Calli.

And Jenny. She hadn't given much thought to Jenny with all that had been going on today. If it weren't for Jenny, she wouldn't have Calli right now.

Though they were sisters, she and Jenny had never been much of a team. Jenny was about six years younger and her most vivid memory of her was when Sara would walk home from high school and Jenny and her little grade-school friends would surround her and make fun of her all the way home, dancing just out of reach, saying outrageous and embarrassing things. At any rate, they had been outrageous and embarrassing to an adolescent girl. She had a feeling that if she could remember just what they were, they would seem pretty tame today.

But the point was, she and Jenny had not been close. And the rest of her family hadn't been much better. Her brother had hung around with truants and runaways and wasn't home much. Her mother screamed and cried and threw things and went off to the Bahamas for rest cures. Her father yelled and put his fist through the wall and drove out to the country club bar to find drink and companionship. In the absence of parental attention, Jenny and her friends took over the house. And Sara went into her hideaway in the closet and pretended she didn't live there anymore.

She supposed they called such families dysfunctional nowadays. She'd just called it crazy, and she'd left it all behind as soon as she was able. Her childhood had been a mess, but once she'd gone away to college, things had changed. She managed to build a structure and a symmetry to her life. It had given her the stability she'd needed, the launchpad. And once college was over, the years in Washington, D.C., had gone according to plan. She'd remade herself and her goals included putting together a family as perfect as her own had been flawed. She'd married Craig, the perfect man who fit every one of the ideals she'd set out to find.

All of them but one. But then, she hadn't known at the time that she was going to need love so badly. It hadn't seemed important that Craig had none to give.

Now, instead of the idyllic little family she'd imagined for herself, she was going to be a divorced mother of her sister's baby. Was that going to be okay? Could she swing it?

"Never mind," she said, pushing the panic away. She was going to do what she had to do. There was no other way.

A sound from upstairs caught her ear and she was up and out of her seat like a shot, heading for the baby's room. Calli was still asleep. The noise must have been part of a soundtrack to her dreams. Sara stood close and watched her breathe, watched her little lips move as though she were dreaming of magnificent bottles of formula, looked at her tiny, shell-like ears, her fingers, her cute nose, her round cheeks. Sara's heart was so full of love, it felt as if it would burst. This was her child.

"Thank you, Jenny," she whispered, emotion choking her. "Thank you for the greatest gift a sister could ever give."

Tears streamed down her face. She shook them away. She never cried. Never. But something was still flowing, wetting her cheeks. Before she knew it, she was sobbing softly. She was just so happy. And so scared.

Seven

There was a light rain falling as Drey drove down the highway. Spring showers, he noted, were supposed to bring May flowers, but this seemed a little icy for that. The slick black pavement reflected the streetlights, making it look like a dark, mirror world, somehow treacherous and foreboding.

It was almost midnight. He'd told Sara he would be back by then, but he was procrastinating, not sure what he was going to do. A part of him was trying to convince himself that he should stay away from Calli and Sara, that he should send her a message, send over another carpenter and never see her again. It would be easy enough to do. And probably for the best.

The date with Gigi had been a disaster. He should have known it would be. Tall and with curves that wouldn't quit, Gigi was about as elflike as a Las Vegas stripper, with the morals to match. He didn't know what his brother was thinking of. He stopped at a pay phone to wake him up and yell at him.

"Oh," Rick said innocently, once he was wide enough awake to understand what Drey was telling him. "You mean she wasn't your type?"

"You might say that." Drey's tone was heavy on the sarcasm. "She was just a little too much on the exhibitionist side for me. I hadn't seen a dress that skimpy since my last lingerie lunch. I took her to Andre's for drinks. When she took her coat off, the band stopped playing to take a look. While we were dancing, she kept rubbing up against me like a hungry cat, and when we got back out to the car, she tried to wrestle me into the back seat for a quick one. Rick, where do you find these women?"

Rick yawned. "I thought you liked them wicked."

"Wicked is one thing. Wanton is another."

Rick sighed. "Okay, so this one didn't work out. But listen, I know this cute little gal who trains seals in her spare time."

"Stay out of my love life, Rick. I don't need any help."

But as he drove through the darkened streets, he had to admit Rick had a point. There had been a time when he might have enjoyed a woman like Gigi. Funny how faraway that time now looked.

Did that mean he'd matured? Fat chance. He was as clueless as he'd ever been. And now he had a baby he had to think about. That meant he was going to have to mature a little faster. He had things he had to do.

First off, he was going to have to face the fact that this was his baby whether he liked it or not, and in order to have any say in what happened to her, he was going to have to do something pretty soon. The longer he waited, the greater the heartbreak for all involved.

Sara was already falling head over heels for the little scamp, despite the way the baby was behaving toward her. He couldn't let that go on—Sara getting in deeper and deeper, investing more and more love—if he was going to snatch Calli away from her.

Was he going to do that? He was tempted. After all, he was the one who knew how to handle babies. He would make a great dad. He knew that with a steady certainty that warmed him. He hadn't thought he was ready to take on a responsibility like that, but now that they had come down to it, maybe he was. He knew damn well he couldn't just walk away from that adorable baby. Was there any other solution? He wasn't sure, and he knew it was time to make up his mind.

Then there was that other problem. If he went back, he knew what was going to happen. They'd been heading for it in a straight line ever since that first look they'd exchanged on her front step. His stomach muscles tightened as he thought of it. If he went back, they were going to end up in bed together, and he knew that was wrong, not only because he'd once slept with Jenny, but because of Calli. And because of Sara herself. There was something vulnerable and naive about her, for all she tried so hard to be tough and sophisticated. She'd been hurt and she was trying not to be hurt again. What good would he do her? What good would she do him?

No good at all. Getting tangled up in something like that would only complicate things, and he had to decide.

So what was it going to be? The lady or the tiger? He drove on into the night, trying to choose, the cold rain falling on his car and his windshield wipers working hard to keep his vision clear.

Sara sat up in bed and listened. She'd heard something. Jumping up and grabbing her robe, she made a dash for the baby's room and slipped in. All was quiet. Calli was sound asleep.

Or was she? She couldn't hear anything, and in the dim light, she couldn't see if the little chest was rising and falling. Was she still breathing? Was she still alive? What . . . what if . . . ?

Calli murmured something in her sleep and the small sound reverberated through the room. Sara closed her eyes for a second and said an earnest prayer, then took a deep breath and tried to steady her heartbeat. This was getting ridiculous. She'd done the same thing three times now. She couldn't go on like this.

Glancing at the clock, she saw that it was almost one o'clock in the morning. The lights were still on down in the living room. So much for the you-can-count-on-me guy. He was gone with the wind, wasn't he?

She walked slowly down the stairs and wandered through her empty house, trying to figure out just what she wanted from Drey, anyway. Excitement? He certainly made her pulse race. He made her tingle in ways she'd never tingled before. So he was fun to have around. But so what? It didn't mean a thing in the larger scheme of things. She had other items on the agenda to think about. She had a new baby, new responsibilities, new dreams to dream. Drey could just go . . .

But her mind flitted impulsively to something else, something knowing Drey had conjured up in her soul. What would it be like to have a man hold you and kiss you and really care? What would it be like to have him touch you until you burned and then take you with his body and...

"Damn, damn, damn!"

She drew her arms in and rubbed them as though she were cold, and shivered. She couldn't think about that. It was better that he was gone. If he came back, she knew what was going to happen. It was clear as the air after a rainstorm. And it was best if they both just didn't get tempted.

She stood before her French doors, which overlooked the pool, and looked out at the rain as it spattered haphazardly against the glass panes, distorting the view. It was time for her to readjust her thinking. He wasn't coming back. She didn't really want him back. He was great for taking care of little babies, but that was about it. It was no good having him around. He just made her nervous, put her on edge, made her think things she hadn't thought before, made her want things she hadn't wanted. It really would be better if he didn't come back.

A feeling of bleak emptiness surged up in her. She knew she was trying to rationalize away the ache. She'd had a chance for something and she'd blown it. Now it was gone. What kind of fool was she to let it pass away so carelessly?

It wasn't until he'd rounded the corner and saw Sara's house ahead of him that he realized his heart was pumping faster and faster. What was this? What was going on here? He didn't do things like this.

The house was quiet and, since it was almost two, he didn't expect anyone to be up. He let himself in with the key she'd loaned him when he left. Lights were on in the living room, but he knew she'd left them on for him. The house had a stillness that said everyone was asleep and he walked softly through it, turning off lights as he went.

He'd done what he'd wanted to do. He'd gotten himself some distance. He'd thought things over. And now it was time to make the decision.

Fish or cut bait, Angeli, he told himself scornfully. *Make up your mind. Are you going to let her keep the baby? Or are you going to take Calli away from her?*

By morning, he had to have his answer. And then, he would probably have to leave.

He went up the stairs, heading for the spare room where he was planning to sleep, but he saw her before he made it to the door, and instead of turning left at the top of the stairs, he turned right and went toward the baby's room.

She was sound asleep on the floor just outside the door to where Calli was sleeping. She'd brought her pillow with her and her robe was pulled tightly around her. Giant fuzzy slippers covered her feet. Her face was young and sweet in the shadows, her hair a halo that caught the dim light.

He stopped and looked at her for a long moment, his mouth slightly tilted in a smile. This was hardly the way she'd want to be seen, and yet he didn't think he'd seen her look more appealing.

He knew why she was here. She was worried about Calli and wanted to make sure she would hear if anything happened in the night. But she wouldn't be able to hear any more here, when she was sound asleep, than she would in her own bed. And her own bed was a lot better for her. She needed deep sleep so that she would be wide-awake to deal with Calli in the morning. He decided he'd better take her to bed.

He had no ulterior motive—or at least, none that he would admit to, even to himself. But when he bent down to lift her, his heart was beating wildly again, and he knew it wasn't from the effort.

She stirred drowsily in his arms. "You came back," she murmured, blinking at him. "I thought..."

She didn't finish her sentence and her arms slid around his neck as though she couldn't do anything else, as though she'd done it a thousand times and planned to do in another thousand.

"Does this mean I can count on you again?" she asked softly, and snuggling close, she began caressing his neck with tiny, sleepy kisses.

He groaned and it came from deep inside him, deep down where his need for her was building like a fire fanned by the wind and beginning to run out of control. As he carried her into her bedroom, she curled up against him and sighed, closing her eyes. She could feel the hard, rounded muscles beneath the fabric of his shirt and she pressed her cheek against them. She had no defenses now. She'd thought he wasn't coming back and here he was. She was too near sleep to put up a facade.

"You take my breath away," she whispered to him. "I don't know why I feel like this."

He thought he knew why, and he felt it, too. But he wasn't sleepy, and he knew what he was walking into here. He knew he should back away, get out of town before it was too late. But he felt the warmth of her breath against his skin and the softness of her body and he knew he was already overdue for the escape.

He was caught up in the web he'd let circumstances spin around him. And right now, he couldn't be sorry.

He'd wanted her from the first. As he'd come to know her better, he'd surprised himself by liking her, as well. And now—he didn't know what the hell he felt for her, but he knew he wanted her more than ever. More than he'd ever wanted any other woman.

Could that be? Was that just the passion of the moment talking? He couldn't be sure. Time would tell.

He laid her down on her bed and spread her silver gold hair around her face. Her robe had pulled open and he could see her soft, round breasts through the gauzy cloth of her nightgown, all pink and white and exquisitely shaped. The sight of them sent a thudding sound into his blood, a roaring that filled his ears and made his breath come quickly.

She watched him looking and when she met his gaze again, her eyes seemed to explode with silver stars. She'd never seen desire in its raw form before. It was very scary—and even more exciting. She wanted to feel the things she saw in his eyes.

Leaning down, he caught her lips in his and let his tongue pry open her mouth, releasing all her sweet heat. She invited him in with a naive sort of wonder, as though he were making miracles with his kisses and she wanted to see more.

"Sara," he said hoarsely, rubbing his face against hers. "If you want me to stop, you'd better tell me now."

She sighed in response, sliding her hand beneath his shirt and exploring the silky steel of his skin. Her breasts seemed to grow beneath his hands, filling his palms, aching to be caressed.

"Don't stop," she murmured, arching beneath the stroke of his hand down across her belly and looking up at him with her starry eyes. "Don't ever stop."

Her nightgown came away easily, and his clothes seemed to fall off him. She gasped when she saw him, as though she'd never seen a man before, and he let her run her hands over every part of his body while she learned its lines by heart, until finally he couldn't take any more, and he came down on top of her and found her mouth again with his own.

It was like water, the feelings they built between them, like a lapping lake that was rising, like a tide that couldn't be stopped. Soft and quiet, it was also relentless, surging up between them, a force that would have its way no matter what. She gave way to it gladly, riding it like a wave, and he challenged it, crashing through its surf to find her.

She cried out when he entered, her eyes wide with surprise at how it felt, and he murmured something to her, but she clung to him and wouldn't let him back away. She wasn't a virgin, but she was definitely virginal, so inexperienced he had to guide her, show her what to do. But she rode the wave with him, rode it high and gloriously, turning as greedy as any accomplished lover would be when the full ecstasy had been revealed to her.

He lay beside her when it was over, lay very close and listened to her breathe. He could tell she hadn't done much of this before, that she'd been surprised by how good it could be. She didn't have to say a word for him to know Craig had been a lousy husband in this department.

He hated Craig for the moment, hated what he'd done to Sara. What kind of man was he? More than ever, he wondered why she would think of wanting him to come back, even for the shower.

She lay very still against him and he pulled her into the protection of his arm, kissing her hair, taking in its floral scent. To his surprise, he didn't regret a thing. He was glad they had made love, glad it had been so good for her as well as for him. He knew they would do it again, but the urgency had faded a bit. He could wait.

He only wished he'd never been with her sister, forgetting for the moment that Calli wouldn't have existed without that. But the time with Jenny had been utterly forgettable. And this with Sara had been a special night he knew he would never forget.

At least he'd learned one lesson. This time he'd used protection. He'd stopped at a drugstore and picked it up before his date with Gigi, pretending to himself that he had it just in case things went very nicely on the blind date. He'd never intended to use it with Gigi. In fact, when she'd first thrown herself at his body, he'd looked at her absentmindedly and set her back in her chair. His mind had been full of Sara and the baby and that was all he could think about, all he'd wanted to think about. He was obsessed.

"This is nuts," he'd told himself at the time. "I don't do things like this."

But apparently, for this once at least, he did.

"You realize that this changes everything." Sara sat back against the pillows with her coffee mug in her hands and regarded Drey with sleepy eyes.

He looked up quickly, startled. "What do you mean?"

Her smile was slow and seductive. "Now you'll have to do the shelves for free. I couldn't possibly pay you."

He laughed and turned away again, pretending interest in the morning paper. This was good, spending a lazy morning in bed with her. He liked it. Maybe this was the way happily married people did it. Funny. He'd never really been interested in what happily married people did before.

He glanced over at her. "You look pretty with the morning sun on your face," he told her honestly.

She met his gaze and blushed, pleased that he'd bothered to say it. For just a moment, a strange feeling flitted through her mind and she wondered if she was in love.

In love with Drey. That was a novel thought and she would have to let it roll around in her mind for a while before she dealt with it. In love with Drey. There was something delicious about it.

She stretched and wondered how she'd come to feel so lazy. Calli had woken them twice during the night. She'd needed to be changed and fed and held, and though she still preferred Drey, she was getting warmer and warmer to Sara.

Languorous. Maybe that was what she was, instead of lazy. She felt slow and deliciously satisfied, and she knew exactly why that was. This was something new, this lovemaking thing—new and bright—and she loved it.

She'd had a few fumbling experiences in her college days with faceless boys whose names she couldn't remember. As she recalled, things always seemed to be over before they'd really begun, and she hadn't been sure what she was doing wrong. And then she'd gone to Washington and met Craig, and he'd been so debonair, such a gentleman, so absolutely ideal, she'd fallen in love practically at first sight. The fact that he hadn't pressured her for anything physical had seemed like a measure of his respect for her, and she'd been flattered by it and terribly pleased. The fact that he still didn't seem to want anything physical on the wedding night and right on into the marriage came as a shock, but after enough time went by, she began to forget such things even existed.

Now she knew what she'd been missing, and she didn't want to lose it again. Looking at Drey, she smiled. He was so beautiful to look at, so wonderful to touch. If only he didn't have that wary look in his eyes whenever she caught him off guard.

Her smile faded as she began to regain her senses, began to realize she was going to have to face reality. He wasn't staying. He wasn't going to be hers in any meaningful sense of the word. This was now and tomorrow would be different. It was absurd to think about things like falling in love with him. All that had happened was she'd discovered a lover and found herself a new way to break her own heart.

Sliding out of bed, she went to the bathroom and into the shower and began to scrub, cleaning herself up for a new day.

"Take life as it comes, Sara Parker," she told herself sternly. "And stop looking for ways to make it so difficult to be happy."

By the time she came back out again, all combed and with her makeup in place, she'd settled down. Drey was still beautiful and sexy and fun. She was still enjoying life. There was no reason to long for things she couldn't have.

"I'll go down and start breakfast," she told him cheerfully. "Will you look in on Calli if you hear her waking up?"

He glanced up and smiled at her. "Sure. I'll be down in a few minutes. I just want to finish reading this article."

She nodded and sang softly to herself as she went down the stairs. She put on a fresh pot of coffee and looked into the refrigerator for eggs. The doorbell rang and she went to answer it. There stood Nurse Mattie, looking large and supremely competent, with her bag in hand and her superior attitude in full-assault mode.

"Hello, Mattie," Sara said coolly, meeting her direct gaze for direct gaze. "I've been expecting you. Please come in."

The woman nodded stiffly. "I'll go right up and get to work," she said. "You can show me where my room is later."

Sara opened her mouth to tell her the room was behind the laundry to her right, but she had already dropped her little bag and was taking the stairs two at a time as though she couldn't get to Calli quickly enough. Sara bit her lip watching her go. There was something about the woman. She certainly seemed to be efficient and she was probably going to turn out to be a wonderful nurse and a jewel worth guarding jealously. But there were other aspects to the situation. There was no doubt about it: she was going to be a real pain in the neck.

Sara went back to the kitchen and began cracking eggs into a bowl. Suddenly a scream ripped the air.

"What on earth . . . ?"

She dashed out and up the stairs, her heart in her throat, thinking something had happened to Calli. But as soon as her vision topped the landing, she saw what was really going on.

There was Drey, dressed only in the baggy pajama bottoms that sagged perilously low on his hips, showing off his magnificent chest and practically everything else he owned, backing into a corner of the hallway with his arms raised to protect himself, and there was Nurse Mattie going after him with a light aluminum folded umbrella stroller, as though it were a baseball bat or a club to beat him with.

"What the hell?" Drey was saying.

"Call the police!" Mattie yelled. "I caught a burglar."

"Stop!" Sara called to her, completely astonished. "He's not a burglar."

Mattie took a swing at him with the stroller all the same, and Drey ducked just out of reach. Looking up, he threw a quizzical look Sara's way. "This woman is crazy," he called to her.

"Mattie, he's a friend," Sara said.

But no one was listening.

"Maybe he's a kidnapper, then," Mattie yelled, waving the stroller threateningly again. "Maybe he came to snatch your baby."

"Nurse Mattie." Sara choked, halfway between anger and laughter. This was completely ridiculous and Drey looked so funny, his face filled with outrage and disbelief. If it had been anyone else, she would have dissolved in laughter. And at the same time, she knew this was no laughing matter. Why, if she didn't do something quickly, Drey might get beaned.

"A rapist!" Mattie guessed as she twirled the stroller like a majorette twirling her baton. "That's what he is! He'll have his way with both of us and leave us for dead."

Drey dropped his arms and shook his head in disgust. This was too much, even for him.

"Ah, come on," he said. "Sara, get her to go away."

Sara felt laughter bubbling up her throat and she had to fight to keep it down. "Let him go, Mattie. I know him. I knew he was here."

Mattie didn't seem to hear, so Sara grabbed the stroller from behind, forcing her to put it down, her expression comical as she faced the woman.

"Will you stop this nonsense?" she insisted, trying for a tone of command but too close to laughing to carry it off. "Drey is no rapist. He's a . . . a friend of mine.

"A friend of yours, is he?" The woman's face was furious. "I see."

Sara sobered. "It's not what you think," she said, knowing full well it was exactly that.

Mattie waved a finger in Sara's face. "I won't stay in a house where there's hanky-panky going on. No sirree."

Sara watched in surprise as the woman marched downstairs, picked up her bag and left the house, slamming the door so hard the whole place shook.

She turned to Drey, who'd come up to lean on the railing over the stairway alongside her. "What exactly is hanky-panky?" she asked him.

He frowned. "I don't know. I thought they were a vaudeville act. Hanky told the jokes and Panky was the straight man." He shrugged. "I guess she wasn't a fan."

"I guess not." Their gazes met and they both burst into laughter.

"I don't know why I'm laughing," Sara sputtered at last. "I've lost my nurse."

Drey's smile was full of cheerful innocence. "You'll thank me for this someday," he said hopefully.

"Will I? Oh, you're probably right." She laughed again, shaking her head. "It's just as well. I have a feeling she wouldn't have worked out in the end."

He nodded. "I don't think she would have worked out in the beginning or the middle either, but then, that would have been up to you to judge."

Sara gave him a quelling look. "Even if I hadn't hated her, which I was rapidly learning to do, she would have come between me and Calli eventually. Don't you think?"

"Never," he said with a straight face. "I usually try to keep anything as strenuous as thinking to a minimum."

She laughed again, giving him a gentle, friendly shove. Somehow her fingers ended up curling around the muscular swell of his biceps and she left them there, looking down at his well-formed chest and sighing. His arms came around her, holding her in the circle of his attention, and she liked it there very much.

He dropped a quick kiss on her lips, then focused back on Mattie again. "She's nuts, but she did bring up a point."

She looked up at him drowsily, loving the feel of his warm flesh, letting it intoxicate her like a full slug of fine brandy. "What's that?" she asked absently.

He went very still for a few seconds, then said it. "I shouldn't be staying here with you."

She drew back so she could look into his face. "Why not?" she asked, suddenly worried.

He shook his head. "It doesn't look good," he said, then he watched for her reaction.

Her reaction was not what he expected. "I don't care," she said without any hesitation, her eyes wide as she stared up at him.

"You don't care?" He frowned at her. "Come on, Sara. Tell the truth. You really don't care?"

She shook her head slowly, almost as surprised about it as he was. Being with him was so good, it would take a lot for her to risk losing it. And, suddenly, proper appearances didn't seem worth it at all. "No. I really don't care."

He grinned and pulled her close. "Check on Calli," he suggested, his eyes glowing with something more than amusement. "If she's still sleeping, let's go back to bed."

Sara shivered, curling into his embrace. He was like a dream come true, like nothing she'd ever had before. All this and a baby, too. It was too good to last, but she was sure going to enjoy it while she could.

Eight

The next few days seemed to flow by on a river of champagne bubbles, they were so light and joyful. Sara felt freer, happier, more impulsive and exuberant than she'd ever been in her life. She and Drey got along so well she could hardly believe it, and kept knocking her knuckles on wood every time she got the chance.

So this is what it's like, she kept saying silently to herself. *This is why people act crazy and happy when they're in the middle of a new romance.*

It was wonderful. She couldn't remember ever being so happy.

And there was a bonus. As she lost her inhibitions and opened herself to life, Calli seemed to do the same toward her, becoming more and more comfortable in her arms, until she was as natural and peaceful—and as likely to stop crying—when Sara held her as when Drey did.

"I'll bet she could sense you weren't used to babies," Drey told her. "If you think about it, it could be a survival instinct. After all, a baby would want someone who knew how to handle babies holding it. An amateur could do a lot of damage."

"It's too bad most new mothers learn the job as they go," Sara agreed. "I'm lucky I had you here to help me."

Drey smiled, watching her hold her baby but his heart was aching. He'd stayed too close and now it was too late. He was in love with Calli. Despite that, he had made his decision. Barring any catastrophes, he was going to let Sara adopt her. Funny, Sara didn't even know she had his permission, or that she needed it. But he was going to let her have his child, even though it broke his heart to think of leaving her. He looked at Calli's little pug nose and her round baby cheeks and his throat tightened. Could he really do this?

When he thought of Jenny now, she was a blur to him. But Calli and Sara were clear and alive and filling his life with a new sense of belonging he'd never felt before. He knew it was dangerous to let it happen, that he should stop it, that he should really leave. But he couldn't. Not yet. After all, he hadn't finished the shelves, and the shower was less than a week away.

Besides, he didn't want to go. That was the honest truth.

Neither one of them was going to work at all. They called in and gave vague instructions, each to his or her own company, when the other wasn't around. The focus of their lives had shifted for the moment.

And though it had a lot to do with the wonderful lovemaking they'd found with each other, it had even more to do with the baby. They spent hours doing nothing but staring at Calli, watching every move, every cry, every burp.

"I've got to get busy," Sara would say. "I've got so much to do to get ready for the shower."

And still she would linger, watching, laughing, loving. And so would he.

"Let's celebrate her birthday," Sara said when Calli was five days old.

Drey didn't turn a hair. "Sure. Why not?"

They had candles on cupcakes and sang to her, then gave her a bottle. Finally they set her out on a baby blanket and took pictures, then they sat back and just looked at her.

"There she is," Drey said proudly.

Sara nodded. "Yes, there she is."

But a little later, a small frown appeared between her brows, and she glanced at Drey, her expert in all things to do with babies. "When does she start—you know—doing things."

"She's doing things right now."

"Right." Sara gave a sigh of exasperation. "She's sleeping and eating and crying. That's about it, isn't it?"

He shrugged. "That's what they do at this age."

She nodded slowly, thinking that over. "Okay. But when does the other stuff start?"

He turned and studied her. "What other stuff are you expecting, exactly?"

"The walking and the talking and the getting into mischief." Wasn't it obvious? The stuff that babies were supposed to do.

"Don't worry." Drey grinned as though he knew something she didn't. "It'll start soon enough. And once it gets going, you're going to long for the good old days when she just lay there and waved her arms around."

"And woke up three times a night wanting to play peekaboo."

The superior look left his face. "Well, every stage has its down side."

She nodded, studying her little girl with love and interest. "Who do you think she looks like?" she asked.

He looked up, startled. "Wh-what?"

Sara stared into his eyes intensely. "Take a look," she said. "Do you think she looks like me?"

He took a deep breath and shook his head. "How do I know? She looks like every other baby right now."

"No, she doesn't. Look at this." Sara got up off the floor and went to a bureau where she kept old pictures. "Look at this picture of me when I was a baby. Don't you see the resemblance?"

He looked, and he had to admit, she had a point. The picture had been taken almost thirty years before, and the woman holding baby Sara had long straight hair and a flower painted on her cheek. He frowned.

"Your parents were hippies?" he asked.

Sara laughed. "Sure. Wasn't everyone in those days? But they didn't go live on the street or in a commune or anything like that. They were too busy backpacking through Europe on my grandfather's credit cards. They were free spirits in those days, as long as the 'free' got paid for by someone in the fam-

ily. It was only later that they both realized that by
adding marriage to their bag of tricks they had made
a bad choice, and then they took it out on each other
and on anyone who got in the way.''

"Nice people," he murmured, thinking of his own
warm, loving mother and the father who was always
there for him. His childhood had been happy and his
adolescence had sometimes seemed a little wild, but
there had always been controls on him that others just
didn't see. He loved his family and he would never
have done anything to shame them or bring them pain.
That was one reason why this thing with Jenny had
worried him so much, once he'd learned about it. His
first reaction had been a feeling of debt and responsibility to Jenny, but she'd rejected that outright. After thinking it over, he'd realized his deeper commitment had to be toward the baby he'd helped bring
into the world. And that was when he'd begun looking into the adoption plans Jenny had made and he'd
found out about the Sara Parker connection. It would
have been tempting to walk away once he knew the
baby was going to a home where there were plenty of
economic resources and lots of security. But he'd
known from the first that he couldn't do that. He had
to make sure everything else was going to be good for
his little girl, as well. And now, he was very glad he
had.

He looked at the picture again. "I'll tell you this.
You've got your mother's pretty face."

Sara stared, startled. She'd never thought about
what she might have that her mother had given her.
She didn't want anything from her mother. But as she
looked over his shoulder at the picture, she realized he
was right.

She paused for a moment, thinking about her family and wishing she could forget them. Finally she shook herself and went on. "But that wasn't what you were supposed to be looking at. Look at me in the picture. Didn't I look a lot like Calli?"

He nodded, then gave her a wary look. "But you're not her biological mother, Sara. She's not going to end up looking like you."

"Why not? She's my sister's, and Jenny and I must have quite a few genes in common. So why not?"

She wanted this badly and he couldn't imagine why. She had Calli. Calli was her baby and would always be her daughter. Wasn't that enough for her? He looked down at the little girl, at her sweet little face and dark blue eyes. Calli looked up at him and made a cooing sound, and suddenly, without warning, his heart cracked like an egg. He loved her, too. What a stupid thing he'd done here. He was in love with his own baby, and he couldn't ever claim her. Swearing soft obscenities, he rose and left the room, disregarding Sara's open-eyed look.

He'd done this to himself. He'd known it would happen. And yet, he'd stayed, practically begging it to happen. Now what? Where did he go from here?

First off, he would stay and help Sara through the baby shower, he told himself. And then he would go. And the thought of leaving these two women behind tore at his soul. But it had to be done. What choice did he really have? He would go and let them get on with their lives, just like he had to do.

The next morning he and Sara were sitting across the breakfast nook table from one another, blearily drinking coffee and trying to recover from the night.

"I don't think she's slept more than one hour since her last nap at nine," Sara said groggily.

"One hour, hell," Drey said grumpily. "All those little catnaps put together couldn't have added up to more than fifteen minutes."

Sara sighed in vague agreement. "Well, she's asleep now."

"Sure," he said with mock resentment. "She waits until we have to get up and get things done. Then she sleeps. That way, she won't miss anything fun."

"Babies," Sara murmured tragically. "Who knew?"

There was a sound at the front door and they stared at each other.

"What was that?" Drey said, trying to see her through the squint his tired eyes had gone into.

"I think it was the mail," she told him. But neither of them moved.

"Maybe there will be something good in it," she said hopefully. "Maybe we've won a free trip to Hawaii and free baby-sitting to boot."

He nodded. "Or maybe they've come up with a pill that makes sleep unnecessary and they've sent a free sample in the mail."

Still neither of them moved. A sound from upstairs brought, instead of the usual jumping up and running to see what was the matter, a collective groan from the two of them, and they still didn't move. Instead, they stared at each other in incredulity.

"I can't believe it," Sara said. "She's awake again."

"Can't be."

"Is."

He sighed. "Do you suppose she's really an angel?" he suggested. "I'm told they don't need sleep at all."

Sara nodded. "She must be an angel, then," she said sadly. "I guess I don't get to go to bed again until she's eighteen. What do you think?"

He cocked his head to the side, listening to Calli beginning to rev up to real crying. "I think I'd better go see if she needs changing," he said, his voice resigned.

Sara nodded. "You do that. I'll go check the mail."

They each went on their respective errands. There was quite a stack of letters and Sara set them down on the table while she replenished the coffee cups. Drey came back down with the Calli report.

"She's okay," he said, his mouth twisted. "All she wanted was to be sure we were still up. It wouldn't do to let us get any sleep."

"So you reassured her."

He nodded. "Oh yes. She's happy now. She'll probably get a little shut-eye. Maybe thirty seconds or so. Think I can get into REM sleep in that time?"

"You may have to learn how at the rate we're going." Sara started slitting open envelopes. "No lucky winners here," she informed him. Then her eyes sharpened. "But there is a letter from Craig."

"Craig?" Drey made a sneer of disgust, though his head was turned so she didn't see it. "What's old Craig got to say?"

She read for a moment, then cried out, a wail of anguish. "He isn't coming!"

Drey frowned. "Who isn't coming where?"

"Craig." She waved the letter in the air, her face white with shock. "His business in China has been delayed and he can't leave. He isn't coming to the shower."

"Oh. Too bad." As far as Drey was concerned, that sounded good. He didn't like what he'd learned about the man and he hadn't been looking forward to meeting him and having to be cordial. He was afraid that, no matter how careful he was, things were almost bound to degenerate into insults and someone was pretty sure to get roughed up a little. And he hadn't planned on it being him. "I guess we'll miss him."

But there was more going on in Sara's face than simple regret. She shook her head slowly, her eyes dark and sunken in her pale face. "I can't do this without him," she stated flatly.

Drey frowned. "Be serious. You've lived without him for the last two years. You don't need him."

She shook her head, staring at him, her gaze clear as that of a fanatic. "You don't understand." She spread her hands out, palms up on the table. "I can't have the shower without him. I have to have a husband."

He thought he detected a flaw in her logic. "But you don't have a husband," he pointed out sensibly. "And I don't think there's anyone you can run out and marry before the shower."

"You don't understand," she insisted. She gazed at him beseechingly. "Everyone thinks I'm married. I'm adopting this baby and showing her off. I've got to have a husband."

He looked at her with a combination of astonishment and awe. What a strange thing it seemed to him for her to need so badly. He thought he'd been helping to pull her out of that. There'd been signs of improvement, little by little. She'd been open and honest with him and he'd thought she was getting over that old obsession with appearances.

"What am I going to do?" she cried, truly upset.

He grabbed her hands in his own and held on tightly. "You're going to face your friends with the truth," he said. It seemed plain as day to him.

But she was shaking her head. "I can't. I just can't." She took a shuddering breath. "I'll have to cancel the shower."

This was nuts. She was right. He really didn't understand this. What had happened to her common sense?

"Don't cancel the shower. You've planned for this and looked forward to it for so long. I think you should go through with it."

Her eyes were starting to look a little wild. "I can't. How many times do I have to tell you? I just can't."

He sat back and frowned. Maybe it was hopeless. Maybe she would always be worried about what others thought of her and live her life accordingly. It was too bad, but maybe it was just the way it had to be. And if that was the case, what good did it do to argue with her?

She rose and paced through the kitchen, mumbling to herself, looking as pathetic as a lost puppy. He watched her for a few minutes, then shook his head.

"Oh, what the hell," he said at last. "Maybe you should cancel the shower."

She whirled and glared at him. "No. Are you crazy? I can't cancel this shower."

He gaped at her, caught off guard. "You can't?"

"No." She looked at him as though she'd never heard such a silly idea. "This is it. This shower makes up for all the years I've avoided my friends, all the times I've avoided having people over and starting new friendships because things weren't perfect in my marriage when I thought they should be. This is the kick-off for my new life."

He threw up his hands. He surrendered. "Okay, okay. Have your shower."

"You're darn right I'll have my shower." She dropped down to sit across from him again. Narrowing her eyes, she gazed at him as though she had something on her mind. "Hush now, let me think."

He watched her curiously for a few minutes, then he couldn't help but ask. "What are you thinking about?"

She pulled her mind from where it had been and looked at him brightly. "I've got to think over who is coming." She frowned, rising again. "Where's my list?"

He didn't know and he didn't pretend to. Sitting quietly, he knew she'd be back when she found it, and she was.

"What luck!" she cried, waving the list as she returned to the kitchen. She plopped down into her seat again and took a quick sip of cold coffee. "There is no one coming who has ever actually met Craig. All our friends who knew us as a couple were in Washington, D.C., and none of them can make it. Luckily, I didn't invite the doctor's wife." Her eyes were shining as though this information were as good as gold.

But to Drey, she was just *too* happy. He was frowning now, sure that something bad was coming out of all this. Or something that was going to impact his life in some way he wasn't going to like. Why he knew this, he didn't know. Maybe he just had a sixth sense.

"What exactly is your point?" he asked her suspiciously.

"My point is this." She leaned forward and smiled at him, her eyes dancing with delight. "Someone else can pretend to be Craig and no one will know the difference. They'll think I have a husband, after all."

Realization of what she was thinking hit and Drey began to back away, rising from his seat and shaking his head as he went. "Oh, no."

"Oh, yes." She blinked up at him earnestly. "Drey, you'd be perfect. Well, not perfect, maybe. Craig was perfect on the surface and he was a stinker. But you know what I mean."

"Oh, no." He put up a hand as though to stop her even thinking of it, his face set. "Not me. I've lived in this town all my life and everyone knows me. I could never pull it off." He turned and left the room.

She jumped up and went after him, following him into the living room. "Lots of people may know you, but why would they be the same people I know? I'm not really inviting many Denver people, anyway. Do you know Madge Devereaux? How about Nimsy Doogan? Elinor Chang? Do you know any of them?" she demanded.

He glanced over his shoulder at her, then stopped when he came up against the French doors. It was cold outside. The pool looked like an ice floe. He didn't want to go out there, no matter what.

"No," he admitted. "But..."

"See? Those are the only women from this area coming. We're home free."

He stared at her. This couldn't be happening. He didn't ever let anyone talk him into doing something he didn't want to do. It just didn't happen. "Impossible. I can't do it."

"Why not?"

He searched his mind for a good reason, grasping at straws. "How about the caterer? I probably know her. I must know every caterer in town. She'll spill the beans and then you'll look foolish. Which is something I know you hate."

Her eyes took on a crafty look. "You could be right," she mused. She looked at him sideways. "Which caterers do you know?"

He hesitated. "All of them. Which caterer are you using?"

Sara smiled. Now she knew he was bluffing. "Meals Unlimited. Tracy Castro runs it."

"See?" He slapped his leg. "I knew it. I've known Tracy since . . . since—"

Her eyes lit with triumph. "Since never, you jerk. I made her up."

He groaned. He should have known. Sighing, he turned away again. "That wasn't very nice."

"No. But neither were you." She smiled happily, swinging around like a bargain basement Loretta Young. "You're going to make a great Craig."

He shook his head, feeling the tiniest hint of panic. He couldn't let her talk him into this. "No. I won't do it."

She looked at him with a flirtatious smile. "This is the last thing I'll ever ask you to do for me," she promised with as much sincerity as she could muster.

He gave her a look of pure, unadulterated sarcasm. "Do you really expect me to believe that?"

"Oh, come on, Drey. Please, please, please."

"No, no, no."

But she merely smiled. She had every expectation that he would succumb in the end.

She worked on him for the rest of the day, putting out little hints, winking at him, giving him secret smiles. He went to the lumberyard to get more wood, then worked on the shelves all day. She flitted in and out, smiling at him in a significant way. He got as grouchy as a bear, but deep down, he was somewhat amused by it all. Still he resisted.

They made love and it was almost as wild as it had been that first time. When it was over and he was still gasping for breath, she smiled at him and said, "Please?" He groaned and closed his eyes and fought the overwhelming impulse to give her anything she wanted. Anything at all.

In the morning, she wrote out *please* with his alphabet cereal. She spent the day doing little things for him, going above and beyond, and treating him like a king. At lunch she made delicious crab sandwiches— he'd told her they were his favorites—and when they were both thirsty and it turned out there was only one soda left, she gave it to him and batted her eyelashes at him. He stared at the soda can, then looked at her.

"Oh, what the hell," he said gruffly. "Okay. I'll do it."

Crying out with delight, she jumped up and threw her arms around his neck. "I love you!" she cried, and went dancing off to make plans.

He sat where he was, her careless words echoing in his head. *I love you.* He knew she hadn't meant it that way, but he couldn't help but be stunned by hearing it. He'd had women tell him that they loved him before, women who really meant it, women who cried and begged him to love them back. But somehow he'd never heard it quite the way he'd just heard it when she'd blurted it out. *I love you.* The words held a power he'd never realized before. The words were very scary.

Her campaign to get him to do this crazy thing for her had gone smoothly and tempers hadn't been touched in all the ups and downs surrounding it. Instead, their first real argument was over *how* he was going to do it.

She ordered him a suit to wear. The first he learned of it was when the tailor came to the door and she let him in, talking a mile a minute, acting as if he should be happy to have this strange man come and put his hands all over him, taking measurements. He endured, his jaw locked in annoyance, and the tailor went away to do his thing, promising to bring back a masterpiece in two days, as long as he was paid the tremendous bonus Sara had promised him.

In the meantime, she began leaving him little hints.

"You know, Craig is crazy about lacrosse. Maybe you should do some background digging on the teams and the colleges and all that."

That was her first bright idea. He let it pass without comment.

"You know, I wish you wouldn't say 'cool' all the time the way you do. I mean, I like it fine when you're being Drey. But that was something Craig would never say."

"Uh-huh."

"And while we're at it, there is something Craig does that maybe you would want to pick up on. Craig always is very attentive to ladies when he meets them. Sometimes he kisses their hands."

"He what?"

"Kisses their hands. You know, in the Continental style." She demonstrated.

Watching her, Drey was stone faced. "Wow. What a guy."

She nodded. "He really is quite debonair."

"All show and no go, huh?" he muttered as he turned away. "You want me to do that, too?"

She turned, only vaguely aware that he had spoken. "What?"

He coughed. "Nothing."

He let these things go. They annoyed the hell out of him, but he figured he would just stay quiet and let her ramble and ignore her. If it made her happy to think she was managing his every little mood, he might as well let her think so. In the meantime, he had no intention of doing anything she'd suggested.

But the last straw came when the barber showed up while he was watching basketball in the den.

"Drey," Sara said cheerfully, escorting a tall, thin man with a handlebar mustache into the room. "Drey, this is Neil, the barber from the strip mall down on Fremont. He's come to give you a haircut."

Drey looked from the barber to Sara and back again. "He's what?" he asked, his tone hard as a diamond and just as cold.

"He's just going to cut your hair a little." She went up close and bent down, whispering for him alone to hear, "So you'll be more like Craig."

Drey looked at the man dispassionately. "No, he's not," he said flatly.

Sara looked surprised. "But Drey..."

Drey rose and nodded to the barber, then started for the door. "Nobody's touching this hair, Sara," he told her firmly. "I don't care if Craig would put a gun in his mouth and pull the trigger before he would wear his hair this way. This is me. It stays.''

Sara read the determination in his face and she capitulated immediately, apologizing to the barber and showing him out. When she came back in the room, Drey was waiting for her.

"Here's the deal, Sara,'' he told her, his voice cool but calm. "You wanted me to playact at being Craig. Okay. I'll do it. But only as myself. I won't dress up as some dream boat you may have in mind. I won't change the way I talk or what I talk about. You either take me this way, or forget the whole thing.''

She came right to him, her eyes shining. "I'm sorry, Drey,'' she said. "Really, I am. I got carried away with it all, and I got a little crazy.'' Reaching up, she linked her hands behind his neck and smiled at him. "Why on earth would I want Craig when I could have you?'' she asked him.

He nodded. His point exactly. And to prove it, he pulled her close and showed her how very different from Craig he was.

Nine

"**H**ey, I thought this was supposed to be spring."

Sara's complaint was a cry into the wind. The evening was bringing in a snowstorm like they hadn't seen all winter. The blast was whistling around the house as though it were going to pick it up and carry it away. Snow was piling up on the pool cover and covering the flowers that had been planted for the shower.

"My guests are arriving in two days," Sara moaned. "What happened? This wasn't supposed to be like this."

"Just another one of life's little challenges," Drey told her cheerfully. He had hopes the snow would keep coming down, forcing the cancellation of the shower altogether. The closer the time came, the less enthusiastic he was about pretending to be Craig.

They held Calli up to look out the window at the snow, but she didn't know it was unusual at this time of year, and she yawned her little baby yawn and promptly went to sleep. They put her in her bed and fixed hot toddies and sat by a roaring fire, watching the snow come down through the bay window. In spite of everything, Sara had never enjoyed a snowstorm more.

She was in love with Drey. At first, she'd resisted admitting it even to herself. But now she knew.

It was more than the sensual excitement that caught her up in its rush every time he looked at her a certain way or touched her lightly on the arm. It had a lot to do with the tender way he treated her, the compassion and consideration he showed her, the way he took care of Calli, the loving things he did when he played with her. He had a sweet, gentle side that he had no problem showing, perhaps because he was so strong and so masculine. She loved everything about him. Even that darn long hair.

The only fly in the ointment was the fact that he didn't love her. It wasn't just that he'd never said it. She could tell. He liked the lovemaking and he adored Calli and he had fun with her. But he wanted more. Men always did, didn't they? He wanted something that was outside, out in the world, and she could feel him strain toward it sometimes. She wasn't at all surprised. After all, the man had had a life before he'd come to fix her shelves. Surely there were people waiting to hear from him. She knew he wouldn't stay forever.

"The shelves are finished," he'd told her that afternoon. "Come and take a look."

He'd done a wonderful job. She could see that he was a real artist with wood. But it was hard to work up much enthusiasm for the work he'd done when she knew he no longer had a real excuse to stay. It was unspoken between them, but she knew he would be leaving right after the shower.

She would survive. She had Calli to raise, and from the looks of it, that was going to be a full-time job for quite a while. She would get over losing him. But she would miss him. Oh, God, how she would miss him.

The melancholy swept over her and stayed. The snow falling outside was magical, but she felt an iciness invade her heart. It felt as though a doubt had become a certainty. He was getting ready to leave.

"Do you want to put another log on the fire?" she asked him as midnight approached.

He hesitated, then nodded and went to get a nice one from the pile on the enclosed porch. After all, there wouldn't be many more nights like this. They might as well make the most of it.

He knew it was time he got out of here. This was like a nice, cushy trap, a siren song in a raging sea. A man could get caught up in this sort of thing and never work himself free again.

The porch was used as a sun porch in the summer and it was wide and furnished with patio chairs and tables. A bookcase along the inner wall held a stack of books she'd just put out, things she'd read recently. He looked them over curiously. They were romances, mostly, and picking one up, he flipped through it. Guy meets girl. They spar. They fall in love. They get married. Wasn't that how most of these books went?

The "married" part was the sticking point for him. Good thing he was young and didn't have to worry about that yet.

Or did he? Suddenly it came to him that Sara might not have the same reservations. What if she were moving from the moment, taking things more seriously? Women tended to do that. Especially women who thought about life romantically.

He dropped the book he'd been leafing through like a hot potato and rubbed the back of his neck with his hand. What a fool he was to hang around in a place like this. He should have known better. He was probably raising her expectations without even knowing it.

He had to get out of here. The shower was two days away. But he was finished with the carpentry work. He had no real reason to stay on this way. Maybe he ought to go. Maybe tonight.

Hoisting the log, he went back into the living room, already formulating his exit speech. Yes, he would leave tonight.

He set up the log and poked at the fire with the tongs, and she sat back and watched him. She could sense his restlessness as though she could read his mind. Tonight might be the last night.

When he was finished with the fire, he came back to sit beside her. She reached out and ran her fingernails along the outer seam of his jeans. She could feel him react right away, as though a ripple of sensation had gone through him. But she saw him glance at the clock, and then at the door, and she knew.

He wanted to go. The pain of it shot through her and she had to bite her lip to keep from crying out softly. He wanted to go. She'd already lost him.

She drew back, her sadness mirrored in her face. She wasn't going to beg him to stay. But to her horror, her eyes filled with tears.

"Hey." He noticed immediately, and he put a finger under her chin, tilting her face so he could see her eyes. "What's wrong?"

"Nothing." She shook her head vigorously. "Not a thing. Really."

But he knew better. He'd hurt her somehow, without even meaning to. Slowly, deliberately, he pulled her into his arms.

"Don't try to kid me, Sara," he told her softly. "Tell me what you need."

How could she tell him that all she needed was him? She shook her head, but he began kissing her tears away, kissing softly, gently, as though he could make up for everything if he were just tender enough.

He'd meant only to comfort, but she responded so quickly, before he knew what was happening, her mouth had opened to his and her arms had come around his neck, catching hold of him as though to demand his attention. As though he'd plunged into a caldron of heat, the intensity of her passion closed over him and he was lost before he even realized it.

She wanted him. She always wanted him. And yet she'd never needed him this way before. And part of that need was the realization that this might have to last for a long, long time.

Make it good, she told herself. *Make it last him a lifetime. Make it something he won't ever forget.*

She put all her emotions into her body, into her touch and her kisses and offered it to him. *Here I am,* she was saying. *I love you with all my heart. Here is my love. Take it. It's all for you and no one else. Forever.*

Her hands moved on him, capturing the pulse of his heartbeat in her palm and holding it as though she'd caught a star, entangling him in her long, graceful legs, pulling his now-naked body into the cradle of her hips, guiding him into the center of her beating desire and driving the rhythm of the encounter with her own passion, her own demand.

He was out of breath, trying to keep up with her. He'd thought he knew her body almost as well as his own by now, but he found himself in new territory. She was a different woman tonight, aggressive, assertive, leading the way and showing him how to please her in ways she never had before. Her breasts seemed to swell against him, her legs seemed to have a strength he'd never felt before, and suddenly he was stronger himself, responding to the challenge she'd thrown down before him.

He pulled her beneath him and took charge, entering with a thrust, going harder, deeper, than ever. She cried out again and again, clinging to him, her body shuddering with the pleasure that was so close to agony. They lay together like survivors of a shipwreck, panting for air, limbs spent and powerless.

And when their gazes finally met, they both began to laugh.

"Was that you?" he said, drawing back so he could look at her beautiful naked body. "Or was that some wild woman who flew in and took your place?"

"Oh, honey, you don't know how wild I can get, if handled properly," she teased. "Stick around. You may find out."

She watched to see if his smile would dim at her words, but it didn't. He laughed and pulled her close. "We ought to get to bed," he said, and she sighed happily. One small battle down. Many more to go.

The snow turned into a blizzard during the night. They were up at two, feeding Calli, and then they watched the sheets of white come slamming down outside.

"Funny how scary it can look out there," she murmured, and he pulled her into the protection of his arms.

They slept late in the morning. They had a lot to rest up from, and Calli didn't wake them. Finally Sara got up and made her way to the bathroom, but neither of them heard the front doorbell ring, nor the knocking.

Drey was drifting in and out of sleep when he noticed a woman standing at the foot of the bed. He blinked, wondering if he was dreaming, and then it turned into a nightmare when the woman spoke.

"Well, as I live and breathe. Drey Angeli. What are you doing in my sister's bed?"

He gaped at the woman, trying to clear the sleep from his eyes and from his mind. The horror sank in when he realized it was Sara's sister, Jenny, standing over him with a look of amazement on her face and her hands on her hips.

"Aren't you the busy little bee?" she noted, chortling with a quick burst of laughter. "Just pollinating up a storm, aren't you?"

He closed his eyes for a few seconds, hoping she would go away, vanish, and turn out to be nothing but smoke. But when he opened them again, she was still there.

"Jenny," he said weakly, pulling the covers up to his chin. "What are you doing here?"

She gave him a mocking look and pushed back her heavy red hair. "Looking for my sister. Do you have any idea where she is?"

There was no need to answer. Before he could speak, Sara came out of the bathroom in a state that was unusual for her. Usually when she rose from her bed, she immediately put on makeup, styled her hair and dressed in a coordinated outfit. Anyone would have had to admit she'd changed. She emerged now with her hair an untamed mass of gold, her face washed clean, and she still wore the lacy and rather revealing nightgown she'd slept in. All in all, she was the picture of a woman who had abandoned herself to love.

Jenny's mouth fell open at the sight of her. "Sara?" she said. "Is that you?"

"Jenny!" she cried, alarmed. She grabbed her robe and slipped into it. "What are you doing here?"

Jenny gave her a significant look. "Funny. That's the same thing this character wanted to know." She gestured toward Drey with her thumb. "The fact is, Jake and I are finally leaving for Florida, and I just dropped by to say goodbye."

"In the middle of a snowstorm?"

Jenny raised her eyebrows and smirked. "I'm afraid you two are a bit behind the times. The snowstorm happened during the night. Your road has already been plowed. But I guess you were just too busy to notice."

"Uh..." Sara glanced at Drey. This was embarrassing. She couldn't help it. She knew her sister thought nothing of casual affairs, but she had never been like that and she wasn't used to being in this situation. Concerned about herself, she didn't notice that Drey looked particularly stiff and awkward. She took Jenny's arm, hoping to distract her.

"Why don't we go downstairs and talk?" she suggested brightly.

"Oh, no," Jenny said, her eyes laughing. She broke away from Sara's grasp and plopped down onto the bed, sitting right about where Drey's feet had to be under the covers. "We can talk right here. Drey and I are old pals, you know."

"Old pals?" A strange warning bell was ringing in the back of Sara's head and she shook it, trying to clear her thoughts. "You know each other?"

Jenny's open face took on a look of genuine surprise. "You mean he hasn't told you?" she demanded. Looking at him slyly, she laughed. "Drey, you naughty boy. Why are you keeping secrets from Sara?"

A wave of nausea came over Sara and she sank into the chair, staring at Drey. On any given occasion, she might have chalked Jenny's shenanigans up to her mischievous nature, but this time she wasn't so sure. There was something about the look on Drey's face...

"Can it, Jenny," he said coolly, his gaze unfriendly.

He looked at Sara and hesitated. This was not going to be good. Sara had changed a lot since he'd first met her, but she hadn't changed enough to take this casually. It was his own fault for letting the truth slide for much too long. It hadn't been fair to Sara and he regretted it, but it was a little late to do anything to rectify the situation now.

He should tell her, get it in before Jenny beat him to it. But still he hesitated. He couldn't think of any words that would convey what he wanted to say to her. Maybe it would be better to leave and let Jenny talk to her, sister to sister, and get the bad news over with that way.

"Will the two of you please tell me what's going on?" Sara asked simply.

Drey growled and started to slide out of bed, wrapping the sheet around his half-naked body as he went. "You two ladies can talk all you want," he said gloomily. "I'm going to take a shower."

"Coward," Jenny murmured with a wicked grin.

He glanced at Sara. "Yup," he said, and turned away.

They sat and watched him leave, not saying another word until the bathroom door had closed.

"Are you going to explain to me what the hell is going on here?" Sara demanded once he was safely out of earshot. Her hands were cold and her soul felt frozen in some sort of slow-motion horror movie. "When did you know Drey? Where did you know him?" Her hands balled into fists and her blue eyes were troubled. "Why are you throwing out these innuendos? What are you implying?"

Jenny sobered, looking slightly puzzled. She never did understand why Sara took everything so seriously. "Drey and I . . . well, we used to date," she said carefully, in deference to what she supposed were her sister's sensibilities.

"Date?" She said the word as though it were obscene to her.

"Yes. Date. You know, two by two, like the animals onto the ark."

Sara felt as though her heart were shriveling within her chest. "What kind of date?"

Jenny looked at her, amused and slightly touched. She knew very well what Sara was driving at, what she was afraid of. And she couldn't imagine why it meant

a thing to her. But she knew it did, so she supposed she
ought to tread carefully.

"It was quite a while ago, Sara, and it was never really... well, it was never really serious."

"I see." Sara's voice was small, faltering.

"For God's sake, Sara, this is the nineties."

Her sister gave her a scathing look. "You may be
living some sort of wild, untamed sort of nineties'
life," she said evenly. "But I'm trying to live a con-
trolled, responsible sort of nineties' life. I may not be
living up to my own ideal at the moment but... but I
do have the ideal, at least. And I'm not sure where this
fits in."

Jenny hesitated. She seemed about to say something and then thought better of it, shaking her head
and looking away. "Listen, Sara. Drey's a great guy.
He never did anything mean, bad or dirty to me."

Sara's face was frozen. "He just slept with you,"
she said bluntly.

Jenny's eyes met hers, then slid away. "Yes," she
admitted.

A knife sliced through Sara's heart. "How many
times?" Sara wanted to know, her voice as brittle as
shattered glass.

"Only a couple," Jenny said quickly. "We were really more friends than lovers. Honest."

This was just too big a coincidence to have happened by chance and things were starting to fall into
place, but Sara had suddenly developed a huge headache that was throbbing at her temples. She couldn't
think at all. She knew the facts were there in her head,
but she just couldn't put them together. Not yet. They
were hiding around corners that she just couldn't get
around herself, and strange to say, she wasn't sure she

wanted to get around them. The truth, in this case, was not going to set her free. It was much more likely to put her in a cage where she didn't want to be at all.

She could hear the sound of the shower. Drey was standing under hot water, washing away his commitment to her. She shook her head, realizing she was being melodramatic. She looked at Jenny and tried to smile.

"Come see Calli," she told her sister, rising and taking her by the hand.

"I'd like to," Jenny said, following along willingly down the hall. "I want to see her. But I really came to thank you for all you've done."

"Thank me? I'm the one who should thank you." Reaching down into the bassinet, she pulled the baby up into her arms and turned so Jenny could see her. "Look at this. I'll never be able to repay you for Calli."

"She's beautiful." Jenny touched her tiny fingers with one of her own. "Do you know how I would be feeling right now if I'd made some other choice? I mean, I know it would have been okay, but I wouldn't have felt as good about it as I do when I know you're the one who will be raising her." Her eyes filled with tears and she smiled at her sister. "Sara, you'll do a great job. I know it."

Sara stared at her, not sure what to do. Her impulse was to lean over and kiss her, but there was this thing between them, this past with Drey. It hadn't been resolved yet. She didn't know the full story. Not for sure. She gathered all her strength and asked the question that hung in the air.

"Is Drey Calli's father?" she asked, her voice choked.

Jenny smiled and nodded through her tears. "Yes. He is."

Sara closed her eyes and swayed, holding Calli close. "Oh, God," she said.

"How did you meet him?" Jenny asked her, taking Calli from her.

Sara looked around blindly. "He...uh...he showed up here about two weeks ago. He came to do some carpentry work I needed done."

Jenny frowned, shaking her head. "That little devil," she said softly. "I should have known just telling him to stay out of it wouldn't work. He had to get involved." She glanced at Sara. "And now you're in love with him," she said perceptively.

Sara started to protest, but she couldn't manage to lie at the moment. "Yes," she whispered.

Drey appeared at the doorway of the room, his hair wet and shining, wearing a fisherman's sweater and a faded pair of jeans. They both turned and stared at him for a moment.

"Drey Angeli, this little girl is adorable," Jenny said brightly, filling the silence. "Don't you think so?"

Drey didn't bother to answer her. His attention was riveted on Sara. "Are you okay?" he asked, reaching for her.

She avoided his arms, but she nodded. "Of course," she said crisply. "Why wouldn't I be?"

"Whatever else, Drey, you and I made a cutie here," Jenny babbled on, smiling at Calli and patting her softly.

"Yes. I know," Drey said softly, his gaze on Sara. "I'm so glad Sara has her."

He nodded. "She's a fabulous mother," he noted.

Jenny looked up from Calli, her face earnest and looked from Drey's face to Sara's. "I know you hear of these cases all the time where people have second thoughts after they give up their babies to adoption," she told her sister. "But not me, babe. Motherhood is not my scene."

"I believe you, Jenny," Sara said carefully, but she still looked stricken.

Jenny looked at Drey, who didn't look any happier, and sighed, shaking her head. "You two deserve each other," she muttered. "You'd think life was a burden instead of a game."

"Jenny."

"It is a game, you know," she said perkily. "And right now, babe, you're winning. I mean, you've got my baby, and you've got my old boyfriend. What else are you planning on?"

"Jenny!" Sara's face mirrored her outrage, and her sister groaned.

"Oh, Sara, lighten up. I'm joking. Don't take it so seriously."

Drey reached out and took Calli from her, his gaze just as disapproving as Sara's. "I wouldn't exactly say I was your old boyfriend, anyway," he grumbled.

Jenny laughed. "I know, I know. But it makes a better story that way."

He hugged Calli close and frowned. "I was too prosaic for you and you know it."

"Could be." Jenny shrugged. "And I was too uncontrolled for you. You wanted a more conventional type." She gave them both an impish grin. "And it looks like you found one." Whirling, she was obviously on her way. "I'm off to Florida, you guys. See you in the summertime. Maybe." She waved from the doorway, and then she was gone.

Sara turned slowly and looked at Drey holding Calli, her own eyes haunted. There stood the two people she loved the most in the world. Drey looked back for a moment, then turned away, going to the changing table. He took care of the diapers and put a fresh playsuit on the baby, talking sweet nonsense to her the whole time. Sara watched, her heart aching to love him, her soul aching for an answer.

Going downstairs, she fixed a bottle for Calli. Drey brought her down and the two of them took the baby into the living room. Sara sat on the couch with Calli in her lap and held the bottle for her. Drey sat in the chair opposite.

"Sara," he said, his dark eyes tortured. "I'm sorry."

She shook her head, looking down at Calli. "I'm not even sure for what," she told him. "I'm not real clear on what happened."

He hesitated, then steeled himself and went on. "I met your sister on a skiing trip. She was dating a friend of mine and he was treating her badly, going off with other women and things like that. So she and I struck up a sort of friendship. We had a lot of fun and we saw each other a few times after we got back, usually in a group with other friends."

Sara nodded. That sounded like Jenny's life.

"You know Jenny," he said. "She's up and down."

Sara looked at him. She was going to try to understand this. "Yes, I know. One day she's deliriously happy, the next, it's the end of the world."

He nodded. "She was going through one of her down periods. I felt sorry for her. It just ... God, I know it sounds hokey now, but then it seemed like making love might cheer her up.''

His words cut her like daggers. She knew he'd slept with her sister, but she hated hearing it. "So you're the sixty-minute man, are you?" she said bitterly. "Dr. Fix-it. Bring on the maidens in distress. You'll de-distress them in a hurry. All you need is a bed and—''

"She wasn't just any maiden in distress. I liked her.''

She met his gaze. He meant it. Still, there was more to explain. "Okay. That takes care of the first time. How about the second?''

His eyes widened. "How did you know there was a second?''

"Jenny told me.''

He winced. "Look Sara, I'm not going to go over every move I made and try to defend it to you. Suffice it to say that neither of us was in love. It was a friendly thing. It meant nothing.''

She nodded. "Does it ever mean anything to you?'' she asked bleakly.

He closed his eyes and gathered strength. "Sara, I'm not going to compare what we've had together with what happened with Jenny. The two are in different universes. They have nothing in common.''

That was nice to hear. But was it true?

"Tell me what happened next.''

"We parted ways. I didn't see her again until just a few weeks ago, after I heard she was pregnant. I went over to see if the baby was mine, and she told me it was.''

"And you didn't know all that time?''

"No. I didn't know.'' He looked at the baby in her arms, at the picture she made against the snowy landscape behind her through the picture window. He took a deep breath and went on. "That's why I showed up here on your doorstep. I used to work for Carter and he let me take this job so that I could take a look at you and see if you were going to be a fit mother for Calli." He looked at her. "When did you find out? About Jenny being pregnant, I mean."

"She was about three months' pregnant and looking into abortions. I...it just killed me to think of her doing something like that. I convinced her to stay with me instead and promised I would take the baby."

He stared at her. "Why would you do that?"

"Why not? I've always wanted a baby, and it seemed to be getting unlikely that I would ever have one the conventional way." She looked down at Calli and stroked her downy hair. "I couldn't bear to think of Jenny doing anything else. So I made a bargain with her. She stayed here with me most of the last few months. I got her to eat right, to go to the doctor. We got on each other's nerves, and she moved out a few weeks ago. But she stuck to her side of the bargain, and I stuck to mine."

He hesitated. "Sara..." he began.

She looked up into his smoky eyes. "I know," she said simply. "She's just as much yours as she was Jenny's. And you want her."

He gazed at the tiny bundle in her arms. She was right. He wanted his baby. He'd never dreamed he could want something so small, so badly. He'd thought he could walk away, but he'd been wrong. Calli had hold of his heart and she wasn't going to let go.

"I should have told you from the start," he said softly, his voice husky with emotion. "I'm sorry. This whole thing is unfair to you, but..."

"It's not going to be that easy," she said. She stared straight ahead, not looking at him, afraid if she looked at him, she would lose her edge. "I'm going to fight for her."

Her voice was trembling. Could he tell? Would he take it for weakness? She set her jaw, determined to show him she couldn't be bullied.

But he didn't try to bully her. He rose slowly and looked down at the two of them. "I'll give you a day or two to think it over," he told her quietly. "I hope you'll change your mind. In the meantime, I'd better go."

"I think you better. That seems to be the only way."

She sat holding the bottle while he left the room. She heard him getting his things. And then he was coming down the stairs. He paused in the doorway.

"Goodbye," he said.

But she couldn't really see him. Her eyes were swimming with tears. "Goodbye," she answered.

And then he was gone.

Ten

The baby shower was finally here.

Sara was relieved. After all the anxiety and trauma, things were working out pretty well. The most important thing was that her college roommates were going to be here to celebrate with her. Lovable, bouncy Cami Bishop had shown up, very tired and disturbed about something and Sara had put her up in one of the bedrooms to get some rest before things really got going. Gorgeous, statuesque Hailey Kingston was here and helping her get things organized, though she seemed distracted by something she didn't want to talk about. And the last of their group, J. J. Jensen had called. She was on her way. Everything was as it should be, and she should be deliriously happy.

And she was. Or so she kept telling herself.

But in her deepest heart of hearts, she knew she would give it all up for the feel of Drey's arms around

her, for him to be back a part of their little family,
holding Calli while Sara held them both in the warmth
of her joy. She hadn't heard a word from Drey. She
knew he must miss his little girl, must wish he could
see her. He might even follow through on his warning
that he was going to try to win custody of her. But as
much as that hurt, she couldn't find it in her heart to
hate him. It was impossible. Because she loved him.
She loved Calli with the pure, unquestioned love of a
mother for her child. The hesitancy of the first couple
of days had been forgotten and they had already
forged a bond between them that could never be broken. But she knew she loved Drey as well, loved him
as a woman loved a man who possessed her body and
her heart, even if her soul couldn't quite make the
leap. There would never be another man like him in
her life. And she would always be tied to him by the
mere fact of his tie to Calli. No one could erase that.

Drey heard the sound of feminine laughter as he
came up the walk toward Sara's house. Snow still
clung to the trees and bordered the paths, making her
house look like an enchanted castle in a fairy tale. He
felt a lot like the big bad wolf at the moment. He
wasn't really sure if he was going to be welcomed.

Just as he reached the front door, it was flung open
by a pretty, dark-haired woman who was coming out
to get something from her car.

"Oh, hello," she said, smiling at him. "Who are
you?"

He smiled back and didn't tell her. "Don't worry. I
belong here," he said instead, and brushed past her
into the house. She watched him, laughing, then

shrugged and went on about her business. He walked slowly through the entryway, looking for Sara.

The house was full of women and seemed to be flooded with pink and white ribbons and streamers and balloons. He looked down the hall, and there she was, talking to a group of friends and laughing. His heart began to thump in his chest. He hadn't seen her in two days and she looked damn beautiful, dressed in white lace with her hair up like a queen. Diamonds glittered on her fingers and wrists and gold edged the lace. She was something special and she looked it.

Turning away before she noticed him, he took the stairs two at a time, heading for the bedroom. It was eerie to be in this house again, eerie to be where he'd spent so much time in the past two weeks, but where, despite what he'd told the woman at the door, he really didn't belong at all.

He went into her bedroom. The suit she'd had altered for him hung in her closet, just as he'd known it would. He stripped quickly and put it on, along with a crisp white shirt, and when he looked into her full-length mirror, he decided he looked pretty good himself. "Even with long hair," he muttered.

His next stop would be to see Calli. She was asleep in her room. The light was dim, but bright enough that he could see her features clearly. He stood over her bassinet and filled his senses with the sight of her adorable baby face. She was dressed in pink and her cheeks were flushed. She sighed in her sleep and he smiled. He felt things for this little one he hadn't dreamed he was capable of.

"I had to come and see you one more time, little girl," he whispered, looking down at her with all his love in his eyes. "I've missed you."

The door creaked and he turned, startled. A pretty young woman came in, smiling at him. Her golden hair hung around her shoulders and her face was bright and happy.

"I'll bet I can guess who you are," she said before he had a chance to greet her. "You've got to be Craig. Aren't you? That's one beautiful little baby you've got there."

He looked down at Calli. "Thank you. But—"

"I'm Cami Bishop. One of Sara's old roommates from college." She came up beside him to smile down at the baby. "Sara is a lucky woman," she said with a heartfelt sigh.

Drey hesitated. "Is she?" he asked, putting off correcting her identification of him as Sara's husband and wondering what Sara was telling people.

"Oh, yes." She smiled at him, letting him know he was part of Sara's luck, in her opinion. Her bold, friendly eyes looked him up and down. "But you really are different from what I expected."

"Am I?" His dark eyes glinted.

"Definitely. Sara wrote to me and told me all about you back when you were first married, and I thought . . . well, I pictured you as the polished politician type. You know what I mean? Sort of an elegant phony. And since she met you in Washington, D.C., I just assumed . . ." She waved a hand in the air and rolled her eyes.

"Ah," he said, straightening his jacket and feeling pleasantly flattered. "Never assume."

"So they tell me." She laughed. "I must say, I approve of the real version. Like I said, Sara is a lucky woman." Her face changed and she looked suddenly eager as she glanced toward the window. "Say, have

you seen a dark, handsome man hanging around outside by any chance?''

"No. Are you expecting one?''

She gurgled with happy laughter. "I sure am. Sheriff Rafe Lonewolf of New Mexico is his name. He very
recently proposed. In fact, it was about half an hour
ago.'' She grinned. "I think I just may marry him.''

He smiled, liking her openness. "Congratula-
tions.''

She nodded, accepting his wishes. "I just met him
a few days ago. He arrested me, in fact.''

Drey's eyes widened. "Did he? That's original.''

She nodded earnestly. "Very. He kept me in custody longer than he had to because we were falling in
love.''

Drey was beginning to lose his firm grasp of reality
now. Openness was one thing, but this...

"I see,'' he said, though he really didn't. "Well,
you'd better give it some time before you actually take
the plunge.''

"Oh, we will. We'll wait at least six months. Just to
be sure.''

He nodded. "That's probably wise.''

"Sure.'' Cami reached up impulsively and kissed
him on the cheek. "I only hope we'll be as happy as
you and Sara,'' she said, turning to go.

She was off like a whirlwind and Drey looked after
her, slightly puzzled but amused that she'd accepted
him as Craig so easily. Sara must not have told anyone Craig wasn't coming. Maybe she would still want
him to stand in. In which case, he'd better not go telling people who he really was. Bending down, he took
a last, loving look at the baby, kissed the top of her
head and turned to go. Just outside the door, he ran

into a tall, beautiful blonde who gave him a warm smile and a hug before he knew what was happening.

"You're Craig," the blonde said, beaming at him. "Cami told me you were in here. I'm Hailey Kingston, another of Sara's roomies from college. I've heard about you for years. It's great to meet you at last."

"The pleasure is all mine." What else could a man say to a beauty like this? The woman had the kind of stunning looks that turned heads and brought in the photographers.

She stood back and looked him over, and just as Cami had, she treated him as though he were as old a friend as Sara, and just as close. "You know, we roomies always did everything together. It was a shock when Sara went ahead and married you without our permission." She treated him to a saucy wink. "But then we heard how perfect you were and we went easy on her." She took another look at him and nodded appreciatively. "Gee, Cami's right." Reaching up, she touched his hair and smiled. "You're not like I expected at all."

He smiled. This pretending to be Craig was turning out to be sort of fun after all. "Are you disappointed?"

"Oh, not at all. You're much better than the stuffed shirt Sara described." She laughed, then her humor seemed to fade a bit. "It's funny how none of us ended up falling in love with who you'd expect we'd fall for."

That sounded like an opening and he didn't ignore it. "Who are you in love with?" he asked her.

Her smile turned bittersweet. "Does it show?"

He nodded. "Just a little. Around the edges."

She sighed, her eyes clouded. "Believe it or not, I made the mistake of falling for a man the D.A.'s office sent to spy on me. Isn't that a scream?"

His eyes took on a look of sympathetic understanding. He'd learned the hard way that you couldn't dictate to your heart just who you were going to fall in love with. "Where is he now?"

She shrugged. "In California, giving them the scoop on my every action."

He hesitated, but he wanted to be helpful. "That's his job," he reminded her.

"I know. But it's hard to take."

He frowned. Funny how easy it was to see what others should do with their lives, and how hard it was to make those decisions for yourself. "If you're really in love, don't let it get away from you."

She cocked her head to the side and regarded him seriously. "You think not?"

He shook his head.

She gazed at him a moment more, and then she smiled. "Come on." Hailey took his hand and led him to the top of the stairs. "Look, everybody," she called out, leading him down into a sea of upturned faces. "It's Sara's Craig. Is she the luckiest gal in town, or what?"

Sara heard her, and her head went light. Turning, she had to put out a hand to stop herself from falling. She stared at the couple coming down the stairs, wondering for a moment if she was dreaming. Drey caught her gaze but didn't smile. He did come toward her, ignoring the murmurs of admiration from the crowd.

"Sorry I'm late," he said aloud.

"Oh, no," she said faintly, looking around at the smiling faces. "No, you're... you're right on time."

"Good." He turned with casual grace and smiled at them all. "I'd like to meet all your friends. I hope we have time."

They began surging forward and everyone was chattering at once. Sara tried to keep the smile on her face, but the introductions overwhelmed her and she made the excuse that the baby had to be checked on and escaped as soon as she could. Drey stayed behind and talked to everyone who spoke to him, charming them all. Sara watched for a moment from the landing, dumbfounded.

"What are you doing here?" she said out of the corner of her mouth. She was still smiling when she'd settled down and returned to his side a short time later.

"I told you I'd help you with this," he said calmly.

She gazed at him, wide-eyed. "Yes, but I thought . . ."

He took her hand in his and gazed into her eyes. "I keep my promises, Sara. Just like you." Then he turned to another of her friends and she fell back, watching him.

You can count on me, he'd once said. *Well, what do you know,* she thought weakly. He was true to his word.

The shower went on and on and everyone seemed to be having a wonderful time. Hailey left for the airport, taking Drey's advice to heart and chasing her dream, and Cami was outside in the back half the time, holding mittened hands with the sheriff she was so crazy about. Then Hailey's law man, Mitch Harper, showed up on the doorstep and got coerced into playing shower games with a group of the women while Cami raced off to the airport to bring Hailey back, barely making it in time. Mitch was headed for a quick escape when Hailey drove up and waylaid him. They took a walk in the snow, and when they returned, their eyes were shining and their cheeks were very pink. Love seemed to be winning out in every direction.

And finally, the fourth of the roomies, J. J. Jensen, arrived.

The first Drey knew of it was when he walked into the parlor and saw the stack of presents in disarray, ribbons torn to pieces, gift tags torn from packages, wrapping paper in shreds. He turned to Cami, who was just coming through the doorway with her sheriff on her arm.

"What happened here?" he asked, knowing a mess like that would drive Sara up a wall.

Cami laughed. "J.J.'s friend, Jack, has triplets. Toddlers. They came through like a wrecking crew. If you think this is bad, you should see the cake."

The cake. The beautiful cake Sara had spent hours planning with the chef. Drey turned into the dining room and could hardly believe what he saw. There was white and yellow icing everywhere, and whole portions of cake had been used like Play-Doh. And there was Sara, standing over the monstrosity, her shoulders shaking.

He knew what this must have done to her. Even a woman not as concerned about having everything perfect as she was would be upset. He stepped to her side, ready to take her into his arms and comfort her, but when she turned her face up toward his, he saw to his amazement that she was laughing.

"Can you believe it?" she said to him. "One little boy did this in about a minute and a half."

"And you think it's funny?" he asked, not sure he wasn't seeing things.

She nodded. "At first, for just a moment, I thought it was the end of the world. But I think I'm getting over reactions like that. What else can you do but laugh?" she said softly. "Life goes on. Doesn't it?"

He met her gaze and held it for a long moment, and for the first time, a spark of hope lit a fire in his heart.

But only for a moment. In no time at all, a small boy came racing through the room on chubby bowed legs, carrying a pink flamingo. In another moment, a little girl of about the same size came racing through behind him, shrieking as though she'd just had a pink flamingo stolen from her. Only seconds later, a tall, handsome man came through, calling to them both, and then J.J. appeared, waved and smiled at Sara and Drey in a harried fashion and disappeared behind the others.

Sara looked up into Drey's eyes again. "You see?" she said, laughing.

He took her hand and a sudden resolve swept through him. If he worked this right, he just might end up with his baby—and Sara. He'd thought it was impossible at first. They weren't really suited—were they? She was so obsessed with keeping up a perfect front and having everything done just so and he was so determined not to let her manage his life. No, it would never work. And yet . . . and yet . . .

"Let's go up and see Calli," he suggested, and she nodded and looked at him oddly.

They left the dining area together and in a few minutes they were in the darkened room with their little girl. She was just waking. Drey held out his hand and she grabbed his thumb with her little fist and wouldn't let go, staring up at him as if she knew, as if she wasn't going to let him get away again.

Still held by her, he looked up at Sara. "I love this baby," he said solemnly. "I want to be a part of her life."

Sara nodded, her heart full. "I think that can be arranged," she murmured. "Maybe we can set up some sort of..."

"No." His darkened gaze caught hers and held. "I want it all, Sara. I want my baby. And I want you, too."

Emotion shot through her like the touch of a hot wire and she gasped. "Are you... are you sure? I mean, you don't have to do this just to get to see Calli..."

His mouth twisted and he shook his head. "Don't you get it, Sara?" he said, one eyebrow rising quizzically. "I love you."

"Me?" she squeaked, all the old insecurities flooding back. "Are you sure?"

He reached out with his free arm and pulled her toward him. "Dammit Sara, will you let me be in love with you? I need you in my life just as much as I need our baby."

"Our baby." She looked up at him and joy filled her, a joy she'd never known. This was love and understanding and a man who deserved the best. He kissed her and she blinked back tears. She wasn't going to risk losing him again. Without saying another word, she reached down and took Calli in her arms, then took his hand and led him back out of the room and out onto the landing, calling for the attention of her friends.

"Everyone, I want you to know," she said once she had their attention, her voice shaking. She was truly frightened. This was a hard thing for her to do. It went against everything she'd ever done, the way she'd always lived her life. But she knew it had to be done if she was going to deserve Drey's love. And right now, that was everything.

"Everyone, I'm sorry to tell you, this has been a giant hoax. This man is not Craig. His name is Drey Angeli. Craig and I...had our marriage annulled eighteen months ago. Drey is...Drey is Calli's father. And my very dear friend."

Looking out, she winced, almost as though she thought she'd be stoned, or shunned at least. But the faces turned toward her were full of sympathy, and the murmur was affectionate, even loving. As she looked from one pair of eyes to another, her bewilderment faded and joy took its place. Her friends didn't hate her. In fact, as first this one, then that one, came forward and said something loving to her, she realized that knowing about her weaknesses seemed to give their friendship new depth.

"It's okay," she said to Drey in wonder. "It's really okay."

He nodded, his eyes full of how he felt about her. "It's more than okay," he told her huskily. "And you're better than perfect."

She smiled, but shook her head. "No," she said softly. "No."

Calli began to whimper. She needed to be changed. They turned and took her back to the changing table, Sara working with the diapers while Drey got out a fancy party dress to put her in. Every time she looked up and caught his gaze on her, Sara felt her heart leap. Her fingers were trembling and her brain wouldn't work properly. She was floating on air, but she wasn't sure there was a safety net below.

Suddenly Cami came into the room, talking and laughing and not seeming to notice that they didn't have a thing to say to her, but only had eyes for each other. Bubbling, she took Calli out to show her off to the others, and Sara turned to Drey, her heart in her throat. For the first time, they were really alone.

His mouth covered hers before the door closed behind Cami and Calli, and Sara sank into his kiss as though she wanted to drown in it.

"Oh, God, I've missed you so much," she whispered against his beloved face. "Drey, I love you."

"That works out really well," he muttered, kissing her between words. "Because I love you, too."

She melted against him, too happy to trust anything but the strength of his arms. "Promise me you will never, never go away again," she whispered.

"I will never go away again," he said.

"Never?"

"Never."

Her arms tightened around him. "You can't really promise me that," she said, sighing. "You can't see what the future holds. But I appreciate the effort."

He drew back and looked down at her with laughing eyes. "Oh, you think I can't see into the future?" he challenged. "I beg to differ." His palm cupped her cheek and he looked at her lovingly. "I'll tell you your fortune for you right now, Sara Parker. You're going to marry a tall, surly guy who won't cut his hair. You're going to have about six perfect kids."

A thrill of excitement ran through her, but she laughed and contradicted him. "No, six imperfect kids, just like us."

"Six imperfect kids, including Calli," he agreed, pulling her back against his chest. "And we're going to make love twice a day until we get it right."

She laughed softly. "That's funny. I didn't realize we were getting it wrong all this time."

"That just goes to show you," he murmured, kissing her once again. "You've got a lot to learn."

"And I suppose you're the one who's going to teach me."

"You got that right," he whispered, and then his mouth covered hers and there was no more need for talking.

*   *   *   *   *

COMING NEXT MONTH

#1045 THE COFFEEPOT INN—Lass Small

January's *Man of the Month*, Bryan Willard, met the most alluring
female he'd ever seen—who turned out to be his new boss. He
agreed to show inexperienced Lily Trevor the ropes…but he hadn't
planned on teaching her about love!

#1046 BACHELOR MOM—Jennifer Greene

The Stanford Sisters

Single mother Gwen Stanford's secret birthday wish was to have a
wild romance. But when her handsome neighbor Spense McKenna
offered to give her just that, was Gwen *truly* ready to throw caution
to the wind and succumb to Spense's seductive charms?

#1047 THE TENDER TRAP—Beverly Barton

One night of uncontrollable passion between old-fashioned
Adam Wyatt and independent Blythe Elliott produced a surprise
bundle of joy. They married for the sake of the baby, but would
these expectant parents find true love?

#1048 THE LONELIEST COWBOY—Pamela Macaluso

Rancher Clint Slade's immediate attraction to devoted single
mother Skye Williamson had him thinking that she might be the
woman to ease his lonely heart. But would Skye's six-year-old
secret destroy their future happiness?

#1049 RESOLVED TO (RE) MARRY—Carole Buck

Holiday Honeymoons

After eleven years, ex-spouses Lucy Falco and Christopher Banks
were thrown together by chance on New Year's Eve. It didn't take
long before they discovered how steamy their passion still was.…

#1050 ON WINGS OF LOVE—Ashley Summers

Katy Lawrence liked to play it safe, while pilot Thomas Logan
preferred to take risks. Could Thomas help Katy conquer her fears
and persuade her to gamble on love?

FAST CASH 4031 DRAW RULES
NO PURCHASE OR OBLIGATION NECESSARY

Fifty prizes of $50 each will be awarded in random drawings to be conducted no later than 3/28/97 from amongst all eligible responses to this prize offer received as of 2/14/97. To enter, follow directions, affix 1st-class postage and mail OR write Fast Cash 4031 on a 3" x 5" card along with your name and address and mail that card to: Harlequin's Fast Cash 4031 Draw, P.O. Box 1395, Buffalo, NY 14240-1395 OR P.O. Box 618, Fort Erie, Ontario L2A 5X3. (Limit: one entry per outer envelope; all entries must be sent via 1st-class mail.) Limit: one prize per household. Odds of winning are determined by the number of eligible responses received. Offer is open only to residents of the U.S. (except Puerto Rico) and Canada and is void wherever prohibited by law. All applicable laws and regulations apply. Any litigation within the province of Quebec respecting the conduct and awarding of a prize in this sweepstakes maybe submitted to the Régie des alcools, des courses et des jeux. In order for a Canadian resident to win a prize, that person will be required to correctly answer a time-limited arithmetical skill-testing question to be administered by mail. Names of winners available after 4/28/97 by sending a self-addressed, stamped envelope to: Fast Cash 4031 Draw Winners, P.O. Box 4200, Blair, NE 68009-4200.

OFFICIAL RULES
MILLION DOLLAR SWEEPSTAKES
NO PURCHASE NECESSARY TO ENTER

1. To enter, follow the directions published. Method of entry may vary. For eligibility, entries must be received no later than March 31, 1998. No liability is assumed for printing errors, lost, late, non-delivered or misdirected entries.
    To determine winners, the sweepstakes numbers assigned to submitted entries will be compared against a list of randomly pre-selected prize winning numbers. In the event all prizes are not claimed via the return of prize winning numbers, random drawings will be held from among all other entries received to award unclaimed prizes.

2. Prize winners will be determined no later than June 30, 1998. Selection of winning numbers and random drawings are under the supervision of D. L. Blair, Inc., an independent judging organization whose decisions are final. Limit: one prize to a family or organization. No substitution will be made for any prize, except as offered. Taxes and duties on all prizes are the sole responsibility of winners. Winners will be notified by mail. Odds of winning are determined by the number of eligible entries distributed and received.

3. Sweepstakes open to residents of the U.S. (except Puerto Rico), Canada and Europe who are 18 years of age or older, except employees and immediate family members of Torstar Corp., D. L. Blair, Inc., their affiliates, subsidiaries, and all other agencies, entities, and persons connected with the use, marketing or conduct of this sweepstakes. All applicable laws and regulations apply. Sweepstakes offer void wherever prohibited by law. Any litigation within the province of Quebec respecting the conduct and awarding of a prize in this sweepstakes must be submitted to the Régie des alcools, des courses et des jeux. In order to win a prize, residents of Canada will be required to correctly answer a time-limited arithmetical skill-testing question to be administered by mail.

4. Winners of major prizes (Grand through Fourth) will be obligated to sign and return an Affidavit of Eligibility and Release of Liability within 30 days of notification. In the event of non-compliance within this time period or if a prize is returned as undeliverable, D. L. Blair, Inc. may at its sole discretion award that prize to an alternate winner. By acceptance of their prize, winners consent to use of their names, photographs or other likeness for purposes of advertising, trade and promotion on behalf of Torstar Corp., its affiliates and subsidiaries, without further compensation unless prohibited by law. Torstar Corp. and D. L. Blair, Inc., their affiliates and subsidiaries are not responsible for errors in printing of sweepstakes and prizewinning numbers. In the event a duplication of a prizewinning number occurs, a random drawing will be held from among all entries received with that prizewinning number to award that prize.

SWP-S12ZD1

5. This sweepstakes is presented by Torstar Corp., its subsidiaries and affiliates in conjunction with book, merchandise and/or product offerings. The number of prizes to be awarded and their value are as follows: Grand Prize — $1,000,000 (payable at $33,333.33 a year for 30 years); First Prize — $50,000; Second Prize — $10,000; Third Prize — $5,000; 3 Fourth Prizes — $1,000 each; 10 Fifth Prizes — $250 each; 1,000 Sixth Prizes — $10 each. Values of all prizes are in U.S. currency. Prizes in each level will be presented in different creative executions, including various currencies, vehicles, merchandise and travel. Any presentation of a prize level in a currency other than U.S. currency represents an approximate equivalent to the U.S. currency prize for that level, at that time. Prize winners will have the opportunity of selecting any prize offered for that level; however, the actual non U.S. currency equivalent prize, if offered and selected, shall be awarded at the exchange rate existing at 3:00 P.M. New York time on March 31, 1998. A travel prize option, if offered and selected by winner, must be completed within 12 months of selection and is subject to: traveling companion(s) completing and returning a Release of Liability prior to travel; and hotel and flight accommodations availability. For a current list of all prize options offered within prize levels, send a self-addressed, stamped envelope (WA residents need not affix postage) to: MILLION DOLLAR SWEEPSTAKES Prize Options, P.O. Box 4456, Blair, NE 68009-4456, USA.

6. For a list of prize winners (available after July 31, 1998) send a separate, stamped, self-addressed envelope to: MILLION DOLLAR SWEEPSTAKES Winners, P.O. Box 4459, Blair, NE 68009-4459, USA.

EXTRA BONUS PRIZE DRAWING
NO PURCHASE OR OBLIGATION NECESSARY TO ENTER

7. The Extra Bonus Prize will be awarded in a random drawing to be conducted no later than 5/30/98 from among all entries received. To qualify, entries must be received by 3/31/98 and comply with published directions. Prize ($50,000) is valued in U.S. currency. Prize will be presented in different creative expressions, including various currencies, vehicles, merchandise and travel. Any presentation in a currency other than U.S. currency represents an approximate equivalent to the U.S. currency value at that time. Prize winner will have the opportunity of selecting any prize offered in any presentation of the Extra Bonus Prize Drawing; however, the actual non U.S. currency equivalent prize, if offered and selected by winner, shall be awarded at the exchange rate existing at 3:00 P.M. New York time on March 31, 1998. For a current list of prize options offered, send a self-addressed, stamped envelope (WA residents need not affix postage) to: Extra Bonus Prize Options, P.O. Box 4462, Blair, NE 68009-4462, USA. All eligibility requirements and restrictions of the MILLION DOLLAR SWEEPSTAKES apply. Odds of winning are dependent upon number of eligible entries received. No substitution for prize except as offered. For the name of winner (available after 7/31/98), send a self-addressed, stamped envelope to: Extra Bonus Prize Winner, P.O. Box 4463, Blair, NE 68009-4463, USA.

SWP-S12ZD2

As seen on TV!
Free Gift Offer

With a Free Gift proof-of-purchase from any Silhouette® book,
you can receive a beautiful cubic zirconia pendant.

This gorgeous marquise-shaped stone is a genuine cubic
zirconia—accented by an 18" gold tone necklace.

(Approximate retail value $19.95)

Send for yours today...
compliments of *Silhouette*®

To receive your free gift, a cubic zirconia pendant, send us one original proof-of-
purchase, photocopies not accepted, from the back of any Silhouette Romance™,
Silhouette Desire®, Silhouette Special Edition®, Silhouette Intimate Moments®
or Silhouette Yours Truly™ title available in August, September, October, November and
December at your favorite retail outlet, together with the Free Gift Certificate, plus a
check or money order for $1.65 U.S./$2.15 CAN. (do not send cash) to cover postage and
handling, payable to Silhouette Free Gift Offer. We will send you the specified gift. Allow
6 to 8 weeks for delivery. Offer good until December 31, 1996 or while quantities last.
Offer valid in the U.S. and Canada only.

Free Gift Certificate

Name: _____

Address: _____

City: _____ State/Province: _____ Zip/Postal Code: _____

Mail this certificate, one proof-of-purchase and a check or money order for postage
and handling to: SILHOUETTE FREE GIFT OFFER 1996. In the U.S.: 3010 Walden
Avenue, P.O. Box 9077, Buffalo NY 14269-9077. In Canada: P.O. Box 613, Fort Erie,
Ontario L2Z 5X3.

FREE GIFT OFFER   084-KMD
ONE PROOF-OF-PURCHASE
To collect your fabulous FREE GIFT, a cubic zirconia pendant, you must include this
original proof-of-purchase for each gift with the properly completed Free Gift Certificate.

084-KMD-R

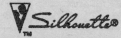

You're About to Become a *Privileged Woman*

Reap the rewards of fabulous free gifts and benefits with proofs-of-purchase from Silhouette and Harlequin books

Pages & Privileges™

It's our way of thanking you for buying our books at your favorite retail stores.

PROOF OF PURCHASE
SD-PP20
Offer expires March 31,1997

Pages & Privileges ™

Harlequin and Silhouette— the most privileged readers in the world!

For more information about Harlequin and Silhouette's PAGES & PRIVILEGES program call the Pages & Privileges Benefits Desk: 1-503-794-2499

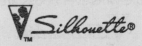

Silhouette®

SD-PP20